DARK DREAMING

PAT FRANKLIN

DIAMOND BOOKS, NEW YORK

DARK DREAMING

A Diamond Book / published by arrangement with
the author

PRINTING HISTORY
Diamond edition / November 1991

ISBN: 1-55773-613-8

Diamond Books are published by The Berkley Publishing Group,
200 Madison Avenue, New York, New York 10016.
The name "DIAMOND" and its logo are trademarks
belonging to Charter Communications, Inc.

PRINTED IN THE UNITED STATES OF AMERICA

10 9 8 7 6 5 4 3 2 1

To P.W.

Chapter 1

The dream always started the same. Meredith was at a party, dressed in a calf-length golden gown that accented her figure and set off her dark hair. She sensed that a particular man was near. She looked around.

A blond man in a tan suede sports jacket leaned against the mantel. He was handsome, but not the man she was looking for.

Now the blond man leaned back and laughed. Another man, one who was telling jokes, stood across from him. That man could not be the stranger, either. He was probably fifty, but was vaguely athletic. Lines had settled around his eyes, and a pink bald spot glistened high on his forehead. The twist of his mouth suggested the cruelty of a naughty child. He leered over what must have been a filthy joke. No, he couldn't be the one.

The stranger did not have to be handsome. He might be older; he might be anything. Meredith would know when she saw him. He had to be here, and she knew he was watching her.

She suddenly sensed that he was standing behind her, at her back, but coming closer. Meredith tried to turn and felt touched with faint terror, like the rise of a sudden autumn squall. The room was crowded with comfortable people who knew one another and who were not frightened. These people held cocktail parties and invited her. She could not remember why.

It was a nearly senseless dream, but somehow sensuous. Meredith tugged against what felt like invisible wires. Desire pressed her, but so did the remote terror. She felt as if she would stand in this spot forever, the wires holding her like a marionette. The blond man would laugh, the older man lift his drink in the glistening air. She would feel the warmth of desire rising, and her breath would become short. Forever, the air would glisten with the tinkle of ice and laughter. Darkness would dwell in the corners of the well-lit room, darkness that pulsed with desire, that pulsed with fear. The record player would play the liquid notes of modern jazz.

Then, at her elbow, a shadow would fall. The stranger would step out from behind her.

Meredith tried to turn her head, but the wires held. Then, from the corner of her eye, and with a surge of gladness, she saw him.

Meredith awoke. Sunlight streamed through the checkered curtains and spread a bright spot on the orange rug. From outside came the sharp cries of birds. The wind stirred the leaves of the tree beyond the bedroom window.

She was at home in her own bedroom, and against her thigh she felt Richard's warmth. They had slept nested like spoons. Richard lay beside her and there was no stranger. It was only a dream, but the sensuous feelings remained—and the dark ones as well.

Meredith lifted herself on one elbow, fighting the dream's pull. This time she had seen, or had almost seen, his face. In all the other dreams, the man hovered just out of view, a presence like a faint tune she could not quite place. The dream tugged, pulling her back. It was not like a memory. It felt more like a scary movie, the kind you watched on television until the middle of the night. Then you turned it off only to lie awake, hearing every creak and movement in the house. The dream felt like a ghost story so real it could live and make echoes.

Ghost stories did not happen on days like this. For that matter, they did not happen in houses like this. Ghosts stalked English castles or Victorian mansions. They did not clatter around fairly new houses in upper-middle-class neighborhoods. Dreams were not more real than this beautiful bedroom, and strange men could not call silently from across a crowd, using a wordless, dark inner pull to bring her to them.

Meredith shook her head. Such things did not happen. She glanced at the clock.

"Richard," she whispered, pushing the sheet from his shoulder. "Richard."

Richard stirred and muttered in his sleep.

"Wake up, kid. It's almost seven."

Her husband turned on the pillow and opened his eyes. He smiled slowly without parting his lips. She brushed her long hair from the side of her face and touched his lips with her fingers.

"I'm still dreaming," he said, and reached for her.

Meredith tried to believe this was the face of the man she had seen in her dream. As Richard pulled her toward him, she closed her eyes and knew it was not.

Chapter 2

Meredith Morgan sat at the maple kitchen table and stared at the page before her. Printed carefully at the top of the yellow sheet was the word *Tuesday*. She glanced at the clock. It said ten. She wrote ten A.M., then quickly crossed it out. *Might as well write down the weather, too*, she thought. Beyond the windows, sunlight made the world seem clean, and a light breeze lifted the hem of the green curtain. Beyond the Johnson house next door, the weather seemed to be shifting. The sky darkened, as if a storm might be moving in. It was Tuesday, ten A.M., and she had a million things to do. Some were even worth doing.

First she should sort and tag the miscellaneous junk stacked in the pantry. When they moved to this house— after Richard landed the Mabton job on such short notice—there was no time to decide what to bring. They simply taped drawers shut, threw essentials into two suitcases, and called the movers. Mabton Electronics would pay, as long as Richard could report for work the following Monday.

That Monday had come and gone a month ago. Since then Meredith had been too busy for a moment of quiet thought. The house, an unbelievable find, was perfect but needed redecorating. She spent two weeks before the movers arrived supervising painters, drapery hangers, and carpet and telephone installers. The best part had been watching all that gray disappear.

The gray had been ominous. Throughout most of the house it had only seemed depressing, but the gray in the living room was so complete that it had made her sad and angry, and she did not know why it caused such unease. She only knew that she had to redo the living room first. Charcoal rugs were taken up and light gray walls painted. Gray woodwork came clean with new colors, and pale ash curtains fell into piles on the floor as new patterns appeared over windows. *Gray,* Meredith thought. She had never known there could be so many shades of it.

She wondered what kind of people could paint the entire inside of a house gray. As a psychological counselor in private practice she had met some deeply troubled souls. The grayness of this house made her think of massive depression and sorrow. Depression happened, sometimes, when minds dealt too long with horror. It would make counseling awfully easy if she could remove depression with one quick coat of paint, the way she had removed gray from this house.

An attorney had worked with Richard on the sale. The former owners had left a few things in the house, but none of them were particularly unusual. She would add their scotch plaid cooler, their stepladder, and a handful of books to her own collection of extras. Mabton Electronics had paid to move a lot of things that were no longer needed. She would hold a yard sale.

Sort and Tag for Y Sale, Meredith wrote beneath the day of the week. She wished she had the energy to begin, but she did not. The memory of gray walls took some brightness from the day, and sometimes, even now, the living room caused her to feel fatigue even when she was rested. There remained a small edge of fear that she sometimes felt in that room. Her memory of the dream caused an edge of uncertainty. Call Halburton, she wrote below the earlier note. She underlined it twice, feeling guilty that she had not called already.

Professor Halburton was now the head of psychology at Mabton State. Meredith had learned that two weeks ago, when she called his old office number. She got the new number, but then a knock at the back door had announced a neighbor's first visit. Meredith postponed the call. That night she dreamed of the stranger, then felt lonesome when she awoke beside Richard. The dream made her put off calling.

Gus Halburton was one of the most important people in her life. A decade earlier, when she was finishing her degree in psychological social work, Gustav Halburton had been the difference between her success and failure. He coached her, bullied her, and praised her through a course that, even looking back on it now, felt more like a nightmare than most real nightmares. Statistical analysis baffled her, but Gustav Halburton unreeled the long white reams of computer printout and, in his gentle manner, made it all make sense.

Halburton was the most understanding man she had ever met. They corresponded after she finished school, and when she sent him an invitation to her wedding, seven years ago now, neither she nor Richard thought he would come. Surprisingly, he had, linking the event with a conference he was attending nearby. Having Gus there made the day even more complete.

Yet now, Meredith was afraid to call. Aside from

wanting his professional references for when she began taking counseling clients here in town, she simply yearned to see him again. His office would be different, but the feeling would be the same. She longed to sit beside his rows of books, listen to the creak of leather as he shifted positions in his favorite brown chair, and watch him fuss with his pipe, getting it lit only to forget it as it warmed his hand and burned out. Gus always became too involved in listening to remember to smoke.

Halburton knew how to listen. That was exactly why she should call, Meredith told herself. She had hoped they could get together and simply talk about old times, but now she knew Gus would instinctively know something was wrong. He had a sixth sense about people, especially about her. On the other hand, talking the whole thing out with Gus might put an end to the dreams.

Meredith glanced down at the page. She had doodled heavy lines around the last letter of his name. Then she had drawn a faintly familiar face, but the face was not Gus's. This was a man she knew, or felt she should remember. It was vague, and the sketch seemed to portray an expression of anger or sadness. She shook her head.

The images of the dream felt near, but she could not quite remember the man's face. She was not sure she wanted to. The dream hovered like a damp fog that the warm day could not burn off. It was there like another presence in the sunlit kitchen, drifting nearby, waiting.

In the first place, remembering dreams was unusual. Meredith generally forgot hers. Those she did recall were dull, filled with minor details she might have forgotten the previous day, or remakes of memory with a few improbable changes. These dreams were completely different.

When the dreams started, the second week in the house, she would awaken remembering being at a cocktail party, in a lounge, or in a park on a summery day. She would gradually become aware that someone was watching her. Lately the dreams were coming more often and, she had to admit, they carried some concealed terror. One morning last week she awakened knowing, even though she had not seen him, that the stranger was a man. Every dream since made the certainty grow stronger. Now the dreams came every night, and each time his presence inched closer. She did not know if he threatened her, but something did. Darkness surrounded him.

Meredith looked down. The ball-point pen dug like a blue knife tip into the paper. Call Halburton, the last item said. Meredith stood and picked up the phone.

Twenty minutes later, Elsa Johnson walked three-quarters of the way around Meredith's kitchen, pausing to study the coupons and notes on the cork bulletin board, and then completed her circuit. "It's simply wonderful what you've done with it, and in so little time."

"The house had a lot to start with." Meredith carried two steaming mugs to the table. "We just brought out what was here."

"You brought it out, my dear. Not we, you. I saw you over here, husband off at work, having to fetch and carry for yourself."

That was not true. Meredith wanted to tell the old biddy to mind her manners, but stopped herself. She wanted to get a good start in this neighborhood. Otherwise, she'd show this loudmouth the door. And besides, the Johnson house was nothing to brag about. The flower garden was untended, and the house was shuttered most of the time. When she and Richard first moved in, they had joked and called it "the haunted house." Then Elsa showed up.

Elsa added cream to her coffee, then two teaspoons of sugar, and finally another dollop of cream. She was plump, in her early fifties, and had a sponginess of complexion that told Meredith that Mr. and Mrs. Johnson enjoyed a drink or two—or three—in the evenings.

Mr. Johnson worked during the day. Meredith had not met him, but thought she knew what he was like. He would be a solid man, both in shape and style, working hard to pay for a house that was not well kept. He'd seldom say much when he was in it. He worked at a commodities exchange, Elsa said. Meredith figured the man rarely spoke because Elsa had a talent for covering any subject like a tarp.

"And after the way the place looked"—Elsa finished stirring and set her spoon beside the red mug—"not that I'm one to criticize."

"It needed a little color." Meredith laughed, and wondered if there was anything in the world that Elsa did not criticize. "A dab of paint here and there."

"That was my opinion." The older woman began telling about the time she had seen the inside of the house after the gray paint went up. Meredith half listened, half wondered how she would get rid of this woman before the telephone rang. She did not want Elsa overhearing when Gus Halburton returned her call.

At the psychology department a student receptionist had answered. Professor Halburton was not in. Neither was his secretary. Meredith left a message and, feeling better now that she had shaken the morning's anxiety, set her mind to work on the yard sale. No sooner did she open the pantry door, though, when a knock rattled the window glass of the back door. At once, Meredith knew who it was. She'd opened the door, resigned to procrastinate awhile longer.

"I said to myself, each to his own taste." Elsa shrugged her wide shoulders. "But I thought gray was odd, what with everything else."

Elsa's voice trailed off. She paused for a cunningly slow sip of coffee. Meredith suddenly realized, with a familiar pang of regret, that the back of her neck ached.

Even though she was only half listening, she had unconsciously leaned forward on the table. Her elbows slid ahead as they supported her chin on her palms, and her midriff inched closer until it pressed painfully against the table edge. Elsa Johnson had hooked her again.

"I enjoyed redecorating," she said, pushing back from the table, "and Richard helped. It was fun doing it together."

"I see." Elsa studied her nails. She took another sip of coffee. "Of course, men become so involved with their work and their offices. At least that's what they *claim* they're doing." Elsa, a chubby and aging woman, managed to look like a teenage boy examining a centerfold.

Meredith reviewed what she could recall of Mrs. Johnson's gossip. At first there had been descriptions of the house's former owners, actually descriptions of the wife's plans to redecorate. New paint went up. Rugs were delivered and dull curtains appeared over the windows. Then, somewhere back in her memory, came a pause expressing Mrs. Johnson's displeasure. Elsa's voice dropped low to remark how sad the house became. After the redecorating, nothing felt right. Elsa had gone on to comment on the colors the young wife chose to wear, mostly black and brown, even in summer. Then her voice fell even lower. She remarked how odd it was.

"You said 'odd,'" Meredith repeated the word that had drawn her in for the next bit of gossip. "You said 'odd, what with everything else.'"

"Especially with everything else." Elsa nodded, studying her nails. They were blood red, but the polish showed chips at the edges. She flashed a matching smile. "Thank goodness I go to the beauty parlor tomorrow. My nails need it."

The woman could drive a saint to drink. She dropped her voice lower and lower, tossing out hints of horror and scandal. When Meredith drew nearer, Elsa switched the subject.

The woman was a pain in the . . . neck, Meredith thought, and felt tension in her shoulders. In this case the saying was true.

"I'm surprised you smile." Elsa looked disappointed. "These are sad events, very sad."

"I've learned not to cry over a broken nail." Meredith suppressed a grin. "They'll look lovely after your manicure."

She leaned back, savoring the small victory, and stared out at the green and yellow leaves of the sycamore. Perhaps this trick would work. If she appeared not to care, Elsa would have to give away some tidbit to get her attention. Not that she cared about the former owner's secrets. This was simply a psychological game.

Elsa drew a breath, perhaps to begin explaining those sad events. Unfortunately the telephone rang.

"Meredith Morgan, please," a woman's crisp voice asked from the other end of the line.

"Speaking."

"Professor Halburton's personal secretary calling, from Mabton State University."

"Yes, but I called for Dr. Halburton," Meredith said. She immediately regretted her mistake. Elsa, pretending fascination with the stem of a sugar spoon, had stiffened slightly at the word *doctor*.

"Professor Halburton is out of the office until Monday," the secretary explained. "He is upstate at a conference. You can make an appointment."

"I'll call later." Meredith was glad Elsa did not know what kind of doctor Halburton was. The older woman shifted in her chair, turning what she called her good ear to the conversation.

"Is this an emergency?" The crisp voice was following what Meredith knew was standard procedure. If Gus was away and a counseling patient needed help, his secretary could be told. "If this is an emergency, Doctor can be contacted," the woman went on.

Meredith felt amused. She had a vision of Elsa throwing her back out to hear every word of the symptoms. She imagined describing her symptoms. Her case was classic. *I have terrifying dreams,* she would explain, *a man is coming after me. I wake up wanting sex. Of course, that part is not bad.*

"No, not at all," she said, regaining calm. "My husband and I just moved to town. Dr. Halburton and I are old friends." She promised to call the following Monday and hung up. By the time she returned to the table, Elsa appeared lost in a daydream.

"Penny for your thoughts?"

"Nothing at all." The woman glanced down at the yellow tablet. "You're planning a yard sale?"

"Not this Saturday, the one after. The people left some things." Meredith paused. "And we moved a lot we don't need."

"Mind if I look early?"

The woman had no shame. She would love nothing better than to poke through a neighbor's closet.

"No previews," Meredith said with a laugh. "Oh, I just remembered another thing. I have to put our name out front."

Paint mailbox, she printed carefully on the list, then crossed it out. "Matter of fact, I'll do it now. Want to come along and talk?"

"Not that I wouldn't want to"—Elsa stood and watched Meredith carry their mugs to the sink—"but I have my own work to do." She paused. "Those other people, you know the ones that lived here before? They had the mailbox painted for a while. Then they painted it out. The name, I mean."

Meredith did not reply. She gathered up her paintbrush, stencil set, and a can of green paint before following Mrs. Johnson through the house toward the front door. Moments later, as she knelt on the grass at the end of the walk, she watched Elsa's plump figure move away.

Along both sides of the street, comfortable houses stood beside carports and two-car garages. Two of the garage doors hung open, but most were closed, like sleeping eyes. Curtains covered the windows. No children played on the green lawns, and none had, even during the month before school opened. No women walked to the grocery. Men did. It was almost as if the women were afraid to be seen outside, as if something invisible but ugly stalked the neighborhood.

For an instant, Meredith felt angry. There should be normal sounds of small children at play. There should be muted sounds of radios as women worked in their houses. People should be leaning against fences, talking to each other, laughing. Instead, the neighborhood lay so silent that she could hear the distant hum of traffic from a highway a mile off. She was confused by this new neighborhood, and the kaffeeklatsch with Elsa had stolen an hour out of her day. It was a waste of time. She wished there were someone else around to talk to.

She picked up the stencil set and separated the letters for Morgan. The box above the wooden post was white now, but it had needed two coats of paint to cover the black.

Most of the wives probably had jobs. That would explain why no one was home during the day. With the cost of everything going up these days, more wives had to work. The women probably spent the weekends catching up on their families, so there was no time to visit the new couple in the neighborhood. Still, it was strange that the women did not even go into their yards to tend flower gardens. It seemed sad, somehow, that they should spend even their evenings indoors. Of course, if they worked, maybe they could afford gardeners.

Meredith remembered her own consulting practice. Now that the house was nearly finished, she could rent a small office. She did not doubt that Halburton would refer clients. In the past she had stayed away from the more serious emotional conflicts, specializing in helping those who had minor adjustment problems. It would take years of experience before she felt ready to deal with really deep disturbances. Halburton would understand that. It required a lot of experience to take wrecked lives and help them rise above wreckage.

She wanted badly to return to work. Aside from the income, the work was useful. It would be worthwhile and enjoyable to talk with people again.

She pried the lid from the can of green paint she had saved for this job and gave the contents a stir. Suddenly, the back of her neck prickled almost as if it had been touched—or as if she were being watched.

Meredith turned and surveyed the street. It was empty except for the figure of a large man who was just disappearing around a corner. Meredith shuddered and did not know why. The rows of houses stood impassive, unaware that she was curious about them. She wondered what kind of people lived here, what their homes were like on the inside. That other woman, that young wife whom Elsa talked so much about, must have been lonely, too. Meredith picked up the brush and dipped into the green paint to begin filling in the letter *M*.

Chapter 3

Thursday night Meredith leaned into the softness of her pillow and felt Richard snuggle close. She studied the bedroom. Checkered blue-and-white cafe curtains shut out the night. A thick orange carpet, contrasting with the curtains, made the room warm. She had redone this room after finishing the living room, and moments like this, when she felt warm and contented after lovemaking, were most of the reason. Lemon oil, rubbed into the dressers that afternoon, made russet wood glow in the dim light.

"You awake?" Richard's arm shifted beneath her neck.

"Uh-huh. You?"

"Half."

She nestled against his shoulder and looked up. Richard's blue eyes were open. The set of his fine-boned face was calm and thoughtful. Inches from her gaze, his chin looked faintly blue, with whiskers growing beneath the skin. She thanked him silently. Ever since their honeymoon, when he learned about whisker burn, he always shaved before coming to bed.

His left hand pushed a lock of hair from her forehead. "I told you about the trip?"

Meredith stiffened. She snuggled closer to relax. "No."

"Same as last time. Carlson's isn't printing diagrams the way we read circuits. Or we don't read them right, one thing or another. I'll have to go up and straighten it out."

"When?"

"In a week or two. It'll only be one or two nights. Fly up, complain, turn around, and come back."

"Only one or two nights." Meredith twisted her hips to bump him under the covers. "He deserts me, but he says 'only.'"

Richard laughed and pulled her closer. "Watch that bump-and-grind stuff. It'll get you in even deeper trouble."

She did not want him to leave. Somehow, it would make her feel unsafe. He had taken one trip already, but that was right after they had arrived. Lately, because of the dreams, perhaps, or else the eerie feeling on the street, she did not welcome spending time in the house alone. She was glad it would be a short trip. The job at Mabton was a promotion, but it meant occasional flights out of town to troubleshoot.

"Watch out," she said. "Maybe I'll scout around for someone new."

Hearing her own words, Meredith shuddered. She meant it as a joke but it felt too close to the truth. If she dreamed of another man, did that count as scouting around?

"Cold?" Richard felt her shiver and tucked the blanket around her shoulder.

"Actually, with you traveling and the house nearly done, I should get back to work."

Richard said nothing. Meredith felt silence grow

between them. Richard had never been jealous of her work. In fact, he encouraged it, covering her rent at her first office until her client list grew enough to pay the way.

"You sure you want to work?" he asked, his tone laced with doubt.

"It gets lonely. There's no one to talk to except Elsa." She made a face and heard Richard's chuckle. He had met their neighbor once. Richard almost never swore, but he used some stiff language after that meeting.

"I only talk to her because there's no one else during the day," Meredith said. "If I had an office, Elsa would have to pay me to listen."

Richard lay silent for a moment, and when he spoke it was with a hint of persuasion. "Suppose there was someone else. Around during the day, I mean. This job looks good. We talked about it."

Meredith recalled the conversation they had before moving. When they married they both wanted children, but year by year Meredith put it off. She wanted to work for a while. Then they realized that Richard's job could not support a child very well. The new job in Mabton opened the topic again. When they shopped for a house, the extra bedroom now empty across the hall sold them.

"There's a possibility," Meredith said.

"I don't mean staying home forever. It would be a year, more like two." Richard sounded as if he had been thinking it through. "But since you're not set up here, I mean you could develop your practice, starting out part-time." He paused. "You wouldn't be home all alone."

He smiled, leaning over to look into her eyes. His gaze held a hint of amusement, but beneath it lay both understanding and want. They had both agreed.

Meredith must decide if she was willing to take the time out.

This was the perfect time, she guessed. Most clients came as referrals, so it would be more natural to set up practice once she got to know people. On the other hand, she would miss being out of the house. But on the other, other hand, she thought again, she and Richard would finally enjoy the life they always imagined.

"I called Gus," she said, changing the subject.

"How is he?" Richard tried to cover the disappointment in his voice.

"Actually, he wasn't in. At a conference until Monday." She looked up. "I'm sorry. I'm not answering your question. I need time to think."

She slid beneath the covers, arranging herself for sleep. Richard's arm, as he reached across to turn out the lamp, shone in the dim light. His arms, all of him, always seemed so strong and useful. Meredith closed her eyes and felt him settle in beside her.

"Time we've got," he said into her hair. "We'll be together for a lot of time."

The dream arrived, and this time it was stronger. Beneath the murmur of conversation, a record player whined shrill notes of music. A balding man with piggy eyes stared with the leer of a fat gargoyle. Meredith turned to see a blond man rattle ice into a metal bucket. Behind him, above the bar, hung a painting of a ship. Wind seemed to drive off the painted sails and to shriek from the painting into the room.

"Are you ready to go?" a man said.

Meredith looked up. His eyes were gray-blue and edged with dark lashes. A small scar, curved like a half moon, darkened the skin over one eyebrow. He looked concerned. Meredith knew that she knew him, and tried to remember who he was. If she could remember, then maybe the shrieking of the wind would cease.

She stalled for time. "I don't know."

Around them, voices rose and fell, a swirl and whirl of stories and laughter. People she did not know clustered on the long orange sofa. Gorgeous people, like movie stars. A red-haired woman, made to seem tall by her hair piled high, moved behind the sofa. She looked stunning in a green silk dress.

"It's up to you," the man said. The intensity in his eyes deepened. "I thought it might be time, that's all."

Time for what? For what? "I don't know," Meredith said again. She had to figure out where she was. "I don't know." The words sounded wrong. Her voice sounded wrong in the wind, which, logically, she knew was not blowing. Her voice sounded as though it did not belong to her. Her voice sounded timid and afraid.

Always before she knew what she wanted. Or almost always. This decision suddenly felt unspeakably difficult. She wanted to leave, but she could not move to do it.

The man seemed to read her thoughts. "Take a minute and listen to how you feel," he said. He sat on the arm of her chair.

The man seemed tall when he was standing. Sitting now, he looked smaller and slightly tired. He smiled at the others and nodded to someone across the room. Meredith wondered how she felt about him. With sudden clarity, she felt afraid. It was peculiar and at the same time true. The man looked anything but frightening. About him the wind also blew.

Above gray-blue eyes, brunette hair curved in a wave

over his forehead. He had gone to the barber that
afternoon. He wanted to look good for the party.

Meredith caught herself. *How* did she know this? It
was as if there were two people in her mind, two separate
memories. One felt timid, and the other felt like herself,
confident Meredith. The man's age was thirty-six. *How*
did she know that?

His green wool jacket and beige slacks did not quite
fit. He had lost weight. It was all her fault, Meredith
realized. She was responsible for his ill-fitting clothes.
Guilt washed over her, but it was like no guilt she had
ever known. It seemed to belong to someone else. The
feeling that her mind held two sets of memories nearly
overwhelmed her.

"How the hell are you?" a voice boomed. The
piggy-eyed man's forehead gleamed under a receding
hairline. He clapped his palm to the stranger's shoulder.
The stranger rose, forcing a grin. He shook hands. He
was tall when he stood, and now he turned and intro-
duced Meredith. The balding man was older, but agile
enough that he might have been a football player once.
He winked at Meredith, gave a gargoyle's grin. She drew
back her hand. It felt soiled.

The other man, the stranger, wanted something from
her. She felt afraid. Soon it would be time to go with
him. The wind would cluster its breath behind them and
carry them away. She would not be allowed to change
that. Yet, being at this party among strangers who did
not even look at her felt terrifying, too.

The man, the stranger standing beside her, would take
her away. He would wait until she was ready, but going
with him was inevitable. He would protect her. He loved
her so much.

Meredith felt sorry. She loved him, too, but something

was wrong, all her fault. There was something she had done, or had not done. She could not remember.

The man turned. "We have to go," he said abruptly, and leaned away from the balding man. Meredith stood and watched the stranger's arm lift. It would close around her shoulders.

The front door, a white plank on bronze fixtures, opened. Meredith felt a coat fall to her shoulders, and the weight of the man's hands fell with it. She felt as if she were frozen, a sculpture of ice, and was terrified that he would touch her elsewhere, that he would not stop touching.

"You said you needed to get out," he spoke behind her.

She could not answer. Then his hands lifted. She began to feel relieved when suddenly she sensed what lay at the end of the sidewalk.

It was huge and made of steel. She could not bring herself to look at it. If she lifted her eyes, it would shine, winking in the dark beneath the street lamp, and the wind would howl. It was only a car, but she couldn't stand cars any longer. There was something awful about them. The car would open its arms and take her in. She would be alone in the dark with him. Something violent lurked in that darkness.

"I do want to get out," she said in her sleep. There was strength in her voice. "I should rent an office. I can start up my practice."

"I can start up my practice," she said again because it sounded sure and good. "I can start."

The sidewalk dissolved as the dream ended. The man's nearness faded, then urged toward her again. At last he seemed to weaken and wink out. Meredith opened her eyes.

Words echoed in her ears. *I can start*.

The room was dark except for the pale yellow glow of a street lamp beyond the window. She heard gentle snoring and moved her leg. Richard had turned on his side, but he was still there. Her breath came in short gasps and she fought to control it.

Her skin felt chilled and clammy, the sheets damp with cold sweat. It was only a dream, she told herself. She had talked in her sleep and awakened herself.

Meredith lay still and struggled to grow calm. Dreams did not feel this real, or should not. She closed her eyes and opened them again. The cool darkness of the room remained. Richard shifted, pushing his back against her. He muttered in his sleep, then fell silent.

The clock at the bedside read 2:10 A.M. Meredith carefully got out of bed so she would not wake Richard, and walked to the window to look into the moonlit yard. She imagined that she saw a shadow moving out there, someone sneaking around.

Or maybe it was not imagination. A shadow moved beneath a streetlight. Someone passed across her yard, and then across the Johnsons' yard. It was a large man, trudging a little unsteadily, but with too much direction and intent to be a late-night drunk. It was like watching a scary movie, seeing this skulking figure. If only it were just a movie. Meredith listened for sounds in the house, and something seemed to sigh from the living room. Except for that, she heard nothing but the terrible beating of her heart.

Chapter 4

The Westwood Shopping Center lay on the edge of Mabton, carved into the border of rolling hills that gradually turned into low mountains. Surrounded by acres of parking, seventy-two shops offered everything from gourmet delicatessens to doctors' offices, from bookstores and boutiques to a health club with a heated swimming pool and indoor track. Westwood was farther from the house than the local grocers, but Meredith occasionally drove there on major trips.

She had come to Westwood on the day she selected wallpaper and paint for the house. That had been a Friday, and on this Friday she waited until his husband's car disappeared around the corner, then dressed quickly and hurried to her own car. She tossed her calendar on the seat, pulled from the drive, and headed for the short stretch of highway to Westwood.

She had a theory, worked out in the night during the still hours when the clock ticked and Richard's steady breathing measured her thoughts like a metronome. She canceled out the first possibilities that occurred to her. The third was embarrassing, and she shelved it for the time being. Now she drove the smooth tree-lined highway and assured herself that the second possibility was the only place to start.

The first possibility was depression. She canceled that out because she was not especially depressed. The classic symptoms of depression—loss of appetite, decrease in sexual desire—simply did not apply. Her physical desire for Richard was, if anything, stronger since the move. The whole question of having a child made lovemaking more attractive.

The fact that she had not lost her appetite was confirmed when, at around two-thirty in the morning, she had tiptoed downstairs. In the faint glow from the lamp under the hood of the stove, she sat at the kitchen table. She ate half a package of graham crackers and drank two glasses of milk. She was not going to starve, that much seemed clear. There was another symptom of depression: waking in the middle of the night and being unable to sleep, but one symptom hardly made a case. As moonlight lay across the yard she stood and walked to the counter. From the pile of receipts and circulars beneath the telephone she extracted last month's calendar. She turned her mind to the second possibility.

The second was the simplest explanation and, backtracking through the dates, she saw that it made sense. In the space for Friday, three weeks ago, her note read: Westwood: paint, paper/pick out drapes, hardware. It was exactly what she hoped to find. In the late night, with Richard sleeping, she believed she had solved her problem.

She remembered that Friday, the last day of Richard's trip. She drank coffee with Elsa, then drove out to Westwood. She spent the entire day among strangers, picking out patterns and colors of paint and fabric, then arrived home exhausted to find an empty gray house and too many chores to even begin. That was the night she had the first dream. They had been coming regularly. Now they were growing darker, somehow more dangerous.

Moonlight was thin when the clock said three A.M. She tried to focus on the logic of her ideas. In the dim glow from the stove, shadows hovered near the walls of the kitchen. She felt a presence, a sadness like the aura she had found arriving home that Friday evening. It was present in the kitchen, but she knew it would be stronger in the living room. It should not be here anymore, she thought. New paint and furniture ought to have chased the echoes away.

She thought she heard a noise near the pantry door and turned quickly in her chair. Beyond the faint circle of light that barely grazed the surface of the table, only darkness lay. If there was an echo of a scream—and for a startled moment she believed there was—it came from outside the house. Maybe a drunk yelled because the bars were closed. A neighbor's dog barked. There was a light thump against the side of the house. Meredith switched on the back porch light. She thought she heard footsteps rapidly moving away, but that was silly. The grass needed mowing. Unlikely that you could hear footsteps, even if there were some to hear. Then she almost did hear them. The footsteps seemed heavy and shuffling, but moving away. She checked the door. It was locked, as usual.

Getting jumpy, Meredith told herself, and switched off the light. The dreams must be causing part of it, and maybe she had heard footsteps, maybe not. First thing tomorrow she would drive out to Westwood. She had a theory, and it made good psychological sense.

Her theory said that she was new in town. For the first

time in years, she was alone without friends or even Richard. She had gone shopping. A stranger's face, someone she probably talked with while making a purchase, entered her memory and filtered into her dream. Lonely children did it all the time, she told herself. Children, even some animals, made up imaginary friends when they felt insecure. It was first-year textbook psychology, and it only annoyed her that she had not caught on at first to her mind's tricks. Meredith turned out the light and climbed the stairs to safety. She was confident that she would spot the man by simply retracing her steps at the Westwood Shopping Center.

Meredith pulled into a parking slot at Westwood and shut off the ignition. She checked the entries on the calendar, then stepped from the car and walked toward Bitteman's Wallpaper Gallery. Perhaps that haunting stranger waited now, directly inside Bitteman's door. Then again he might not. Meredith smiled, but without much pleasure, as she thought of the third possibility. The third possibility was to go through dream enactment, a psychological technique. She would try dream enactment only if this trick failed. She stepped to the sidewalk, sure she would succeed.

Ninety minutes later, concealed between plumbing fixtures and a rack of plastic pipes in Fisher's Better Hardware, Meredith felt her confidence fade. She had been to three stores. This was the last. She had dawdled in busy aisles, vaguely feeling like a housewife who shoplifted for thrills. In each store she waited to see every man on the staff.

She saw tall men, thin men, short men, and chubby ones. None was the stranger. No one who had asked to help her or who cast admiring glances her way had those piercing gray-blue eyes. She remembered the stranger's voice. Hearing it again in her mind felt terrifying, yet she knew rationally that it was a thoroughly normal voice. It was pleasant; gentle but deep. She had not heard that voice this morning.

She flipped idly through the plastic signs lodged in a wire rack. They offered to help her sell her house, her car, her cat, or warn her neighbors of a vicious dog. Occasionally she hazarded a glance past the rack where salesmen brought customers to the cash register. She was beginning to lose hope.

"Mrs. Morgan?"

Meredith faced a fragile, spindly boy. He smiled. Guiltily Meredith realized she had been half expecting a uniformed security guard, alerted to her presence by the store manager.

"I'm Mrs. Morgan, but . . ." Meredith stopped. The boy seemed at ease and familiar. She remembered that he had waited on her three weeks ago.

"How's the house? All fixed up?"

"The house is fine." She regained her calm. "How did you know my name?"

"Oh, that." The boy flashed a grin and pushed a stray tuft of hair from his forehead. "I go over the checks—the big ones, mostly—and try to remember faces. Makes more sales." The boy beamed and thrust his fists into the pockets of his red customer-service jacket. "Help you with anything today?"

Meredith realized she still held the edge of the black wire rack. "I need a sign for a yard sale," she said quickly. "Something I can put on the lawn."

"Sure thing." The boy flipped through the assortment and pulled out a red-and-black rectangle. "Put the time and date down here. Use a felt tip. That way you can wipe it off, use it again."

Meredith followed him to the register and watched him write up the sale. He seemed so eager to please, she decided to take a chance.

"When I was here the last time, I thought I saw a friend from college. Are all your regular salesmen working today?"

The boy slipped the sign into a red-and-gold bag. He stapled the receipt. "Sure thing. What does your friend look like?"

Meredith described the stranger, uncomfortable with the task of making him sound like anyone else instead of a terrifying phantom. She figured he was over six feet, a slender man with brown hair. "He wears his clothes too big. At least he did in college. And he has a scar." With a fingernail, she traced an arc above her eyebrow.

"Not here," the boy immediately replied. He handed her the package. "I know the guys around here. Do you remember him wearing a red coat?"

"I don't, that's true. Must have been another store."

"Can't be. Not around here anyway." The boy folded his arms over his chest. "I got elected to the retail workers union last year. Treasurer." He pointed to a patch above his jacket pocket. "If your friend is here, I'd know him. Guess I've tracked down every salesman in Westwood. Collecting dues." He mugged a rueful smile.

"Oh well, must have been somewhere else."

"Sure thing. And let me know when I can help you again." He followed her to the door and held it open as she passed.

Meredith stepped onto the brightly lit concourse. She felt angry at the boy, but he had to be telling the truth. If he was right, then possibility number two could be canceled out. She surveyed the wide avenue, its expanse bordered by glaring plate glass. There was nowhere else to look.

Meredith walked aimlessly, watching faces pass. Women moved along the sidewalks, carrying colorful packages and pushing baby strollers. Few men came to the stores on a weekday. Beneath the tapping of heels and the squeal of rubber-soled shoes, she heard doors open and close and soft music coming from speakers high in the ceiling. Bright colors vied for her attention from store windows. Meredith fought to ignore them.

There had to be an explanation. The only idea left said that somewhere deep in her mind, beneath life's secure exterior, lay an unacknowledged need. It expressed its urgent hunger in dreams. The answer to finding out that need was the last alternative, to act out the dream. Meredith did not like the prospect, but any other alternative was pure hocus-pocus. This was not the Middle Ages, she told herself. People no longer believed in ghostly presences sneaking up on you in your sleep to steal your soul. That sort of thing went out with the witch-hunts.

Meredith pulled the hardware store package to her chest and closed her arms over it. She quelled a shiver of distaste. She needed dream interpretation, not an exorcism, but dream enactment could be frightening, too. She had not acted out a dream since her studies in college. Over the years she occasionally led a client in the therapy, but it always made her uncomfortable. Yet dream enactment was next. She looked up.

To her surprise, she realized she had come to stand away from the crowd, facing a dress shop window. On a mannequin a chocolate brown shirtwaist dress hung limply beneath a spotlight, like the memory of an austere girlhood. It was made of nylon. Small white buttons drew a strict line down the blouse. At the waist, fabric gathered to flare out for the skirt's folds.

A mirror, installed at the rear of the window, reflected a darkening sky and also showed the back of the dress. Meredith felt a breath of wind on her hair and shoulders. She looked at herself in that mirror, a self framed by darkness and a teasing wind. The reflection in the glass prompted a quick glance from side to side to discover another woman. No one was there. This was her own face.

She did not look the way she felt. She looked tired, like a woman worn with grief. Her skin was pale, her face a sagging blur. Her mind felt cluttered, as though somebody else were inside it, somebody who felt afraid of even the wind. That somebody had a personality nothing like hers. Meredith shook her head, trying to clear her thoughts. The other person was still there. That person was not trying to control her, yet she felt her vision change.

The lime-green jumpsuit she had chosen to wear that morning seemed garish and loud. Surely it made her look as though she were dressed in someone else's clothing; a small, insignificant woman trying to attract more attention than she deserved. She wondered why bright green had always been her favorite color.

Meredith glanced at the dress again. A tag on the sleeve said it was on sale. The whiteness of the tag leaped toward her, bright and insistent against the dark shade of the fabric and the sky, which even now continued to darken in the mirror. She checked her wallet and found she had enough. Besides, a new dress would make her feel better. She pushed open the yellow door of the shop.

A salesgirl looked up, startled at the suddenness of Meredith's entry. "Something I can help you find?"

For an instant Meredith felt uncertain about how to answer. The salesgirl smiled—a frightening smile, in a way—red lips parting to show a slash of white teeth. Meredith tried to remember what to say.

"Do you have that in a nine?" She pointed timidly to the window. What was *wrong* with her? She was not a timid woman.

"I'll check." As if sensing her urgency, the salesgirl hurried toward the back of the store. Meredith looked at the crowded tables and aisles. Summer dresses were on sale, bright yellows, oranges, fancy Hawaiian prints, and bold flowery patterns being closed out with the coming of winter. On any other day, the colorful displays would have tempted her. Today their blaring tones seemed in poor taste. The colors and fabrics blurred and swam in her vision, a frightening kaleidoscope closing in, threatening to surround her.

"There you go. Try it on?"

"I'm sure it will fit," Meredith said apologetically. She pulled out her wallet. She could not bear to stay here or anywhere out in public much longer. She could not do it; not today, when this darkness, a whirlpool of gloom, wanted to tug her down.

The girl looked at her oddly. She shrugged. "Cash or charge?"

"Cash," Meredith said, and felt like weeping. She pushed two bills across the counter. She watched as the dress was folded and eased into a bag. Beyond the windows the sky had turned a deeper black. Timidity made her shudder, and she thought that rain would fill the sky with tears.

Ten minutes later cars honked and fled the parking lot as shoppers tried to get home before the storm. Meredith sat safe in her car. She pulled back the wrapping and spread the brown dress over the car seat. The tiny buttons suggested modesty, and the white Peter Pan collar was made for a woman who wanted to be inconspicuous. She had never worn anything like it.

Meredith glanced in the rearview mirror. Her own dark, attractive features looked anything but inconspicuous.

She studied her face and felt annoyed. The miasma of panic was past, yet it seemed she had been compelled to buy this dress. Compelled. The minute she reached the safety of the car, that terrifying impulse evaporated. She nervously searched for an explanation.

Shops probably installed those unflattering mirrors deliberately. A woman passed, saw herself looking awful, then rushed right in to buy something. She had fallen for an old trick.

Meredith tossed the package over her shoulder into the backseat. Thirty dollars and on sale; they would not take it back. If she left the tags on, she might get twenty for it at the yard sale.

Chapter 5

Meredith unlocked the front door and stepped inside just as the sky let loose the first torrent of the storm. It cast a curtain behind her as she swung the door shut and locked it.

Driving from Westwood, she had fled dark clouds, yet they seemed to follow. Now the living room lay in half darkness. She flicked on a table lamp and hurried into the kitchen.

If she was going to do dream therapy, there was no sense in putting it off. She did not want to spend another night with that stranger. Besides, it was clear from what happened at Westwood that these dreams must be affecting her waking life as well. If she were fully rested and alert, she told herself, she never would have bought that hideous dress. She put on a pot of water, tossed the dress bag into the pantry, then waited for the kettle to whistle before mixing a cup of cocoa. As an afterthought, she mixed a second cup. That would be for the stranger. If she was going to act out this drama, there was no sense going halfway.

She carried both mugs to the living room and set one on the end table before settling onto the sofa.

"Okay, mister," she said aloud, "you and I are going to have a talk."

The words echoed in the empty air. They sounded as ridiculous as she had feared. Even worse, the approach was all wrong and she knew it. The essence of unfolding a dream was playing all the parts, being patient and sensitive to the unconscious material. "Pretend you are each person in the dream," she always instructed her clients. "Get to know how everyone feels."

She set her mug on the coffee table and watched steam climb into the air. The setting was too bright. She switched off the light, and gray-green storm light fell over the room.

"I apologize." She addressed the empty armchair again. "I suppose we can have a quiet chat." She paused, fighting her discomfort. Though alone, she felt embarrassed. Above her, she heard rain drum on the roof of the second floor. It beat a tattoo on the patio's metal awning. She tried her voice again, and this time, at least, it sounded more sensible.

"You come to me in dreams. I know you from somewhere. I understand that you care for me. You want to help. You are part of my mind." Meredith paused, forcing the necessary words. "I feel afraid of you. Why should I be afraid of you?"

There. It was out. She stood and walked to the armchair. Now she must take the stranger's role, reach into her thoughts, and discover how he felt. If she could acknowledge and express the need behind the dreams, they would pass.

Meredith sat and tried to imagine that she was the man. Her mind had created him, he was part of her. She should be able to imagine him as herself, in only the very thought did not feel utterly terrifying. Meredith felt a wave of panic rising up, like a hand at her throat, but she pushed the sensation down. She simply had to try, that was all. Both her mind and the power of those dreams demanded it.

It would not work. She sensed that the man would not sit in the armchair in this spot. It had to be closer to the couch.

Meredith stood and pushed the heavy chair. It slid easily over the carpet, and she stepped back to look at it. She had pushed it too far. She leaned against it again, moving a few inches. That felt better. She congratulated herself. The man's presence, as chilling as it was to imagine, had begun to feel natural.

She settled back on the sofa to try again. "I said you frighten me. That's not completely true." She paused, seeking the words. "I am afraid, but I also feel pulled toward you, whoever you are. It's like an attraction, but darker. More dangerous. I may have seen you some-where, but now you're part of me. I feel . . ." She let the words trail off.

She did feel, suddenly and spontaneously, that she was tied to the stranger. A powerful, invisible bond held her to him. And he was also bound to her. It should be a strong bond, but somehow it felt filled with tears. His sorrow swirled around her as if they were living sepa-rately in the silent air.

Meredith stood and took a step toward the chair. She would take his place now to get in touch with those feelings. Then she stopped.

The man was sitting in the armchair.

He wasn't doing anything to threaten her, but the sight of his face sent terror through her veins. Shadows seemed to sway on the walls, like echoes of pain.

Meredith drew back and sat abruptly on the sofa. It was not, she tried to persuade herself, that she actually *saw* him. With the chair turned away from the windows, it was enfolded in shadows. The man's profile seemed a bit nebulous, like a shadow whose outlines cut it off too sharply from the surrounding air. She thought of turning on the light, but the dream enactment had begun to work. If she broke it now she would destroy the illusion. And, she told herself defiantly, it *definitely* was an illusion.

It was not so much the apparition in the gauzy light that held her back. What stopped her was the absolute certainty that she was no longer alone in the room. She was stunned. She felt physical fear, but not fear of death. It was the fear of attack, of physical assault; the fear of hands tearing at her clothes. Hands that would bruise, and a harsh voice that would grunt like a beast.

But it was not his hands that she feared. She almost wanted to touch his hands. Yet if she did, if he were truly there to touch, she would cross a boundary she might not be able to get back across. There was terror in the knowledge of his unreality, but if he became real it would be far worse.

She listened. Gusts of wind tried the seals of the windows. Rain tapped at the window, like fingernails scratching the glass. She was not yet terrified, but feared that soon she would be.

"Won't you please come to me," he said gently. He lifted his arm in the space that separated them. A shadow moved on the wall, but it was not her shadow, and it could not be his.

Meredith stared. The voice seemed to come from the direction of the armchair, but from no spot she could pinpoint. It insinuated itself into the air, like a faint perfume. It was like the fruitlike fragrance that now hung in the air.

"I smell that," she said aloud. "I smell after-shave."

"I put it on for you."

Meredith rose slowly and edged away from the sofa. She fought her panic, struggling to recall if dream therapy should be allowed to go on like this. She knew the answer, but the knowledge felt far away, locked in a secret closet of her mind. She should stop. This was going too fast. Every ounce of good sense inside her knew it, and every muscle, every inch of flesh, every cell knew that she wanted to continue.

"Where are you going?" He was disappointed. The smell of after-shave hung in the air, heavy and sensuous. She wanted to run from it, wanted to push open the front door and run into the rain. But the front door was locked, and a part of her also wanted to stay. A peculiar lethargy gripped her, a heavy weight of helplessness that hardly allowed her to move. She felt drugged by a dream that would not pass even when the dreamer woke.

"I'll turn on the heat," she said. She reached the far living room wall and her shoulder nudged the thermostat. "I feel cold."

It was true. Chill air surrounded her and seemed to penetrate to her marrow. It ran like ice water. Cold seemed to lie like a sheen on gray walls. She fought for courage, then turned. She lifted her fingers to the thermostat.

At once she felt better. The metal dial was real and cold to the touch. The first fall storm had arrived, she remembered. The weather report had predicted a drop in temperatures. That was why it was cold in the house.

These ordinary thoughts offered reassuring hope. It was only a storm, after all, as predictable as the seasons.

She was Meredith Morgan, and she lived here with her husband. This was only a game she was playing, and it had become too real. She had frightened herself. Meredith leaned her forehead against the cool wall and felt the race of her pulse slow. The man's presence was only pretending. She did not have to be afraid.

Beneath the mutter of the storm, she heard a reassuring click from the basement as the furnace kicked on. She was behaving ridiculously. The dim light, the storm, the sleepless night had her spooked. She had only spoken the man's words, not heard them.

Heat from the vent began to eddy around her ankles. *May as well get on with it,* she decided. She had come this far.

Meredith turned slowly, watching the chair in spite of herself. Shadows hung over it. From where she stood, they seemed to change shapes, as if the man had leaned forward. She tried to tell herself she was alone in the room, but once again the certainty gripped her. It was an awareness deeper than all her reasoning, a conviction she needed no proof to trust. *Are you there?* she wanted to say. She could not speak. Warm air moved against her legs, but her skin prickled with cold. She shivered.

"Come and sit down." The shadow seemed to shift backward in the chair. "You'll feel warmer on the couch."

Meredith did not want to move, but she watched in wonder as, involuntarily, her body obeyed. She felt drawn by invisible cords, her arms heavy, her body a weight to be dragged toward the void of darkness that only he inhabited. The stranger's voice spoke on, calm and sure. *He knows what I need,* Meredith thought. *He has always looked after me.* She tried to question her thoughts, but resisting them felt as impossible as resisting the cords that pulled her forward. At last she reached the couch and the cords let go. She had entered the darkness, but he was there. His presence was frightening, yet without him she would be utterly alone in this freezing void of emptiness.

The man waited until she was seated before he spoke.

"You said you were afraid. We could talk it over. It might pass."

"I try," Meredith said, her voice shaking.

"Do you still love me?"

Meredith wanted to feel amazed. She could not. The words sounded natural, as if they had spoken them to each other every day for years.

She searched her feelings. She found, deep beneath the frozen silence and the lethargy it carried, a circle of warmth for him. It was like the warmth from someone else's memory. It was not from her memory, but it was real. It lay like a calm pool hidden deep in the caverns of a mountain.

"I think so."

Disappointment eddied toward her across the dark air.

"I do," she said, speaking again. The words felt true. "I do love you. I just can't show it."

"That's good. I worry sometimes."

Meredith struggled to form an image of the man. The shadows surrounding the chair were formless, but if he was there, it he was truly present in her mind, she ought to be able to see him. She closed her eyes and searched for a picture of how he looked, seated not five steps away in the yellow armchair.

But the chair was not yellow. Not now.

Gradually the vision took shape. The man's face remained blurry, but she sensed his position against the pale gray fabric of the chair. His hands lay folded in his lap. He wore a bright blue shirt and brown trousers. His legs were extended and the pant cuffs trailed along the charcoal carpet.

Meredith's eyelids fluttered open. In the vision, the room seemed changed. Now it gradually became familiar; gray fading away, colors emerging exactly as she had planned them. Only the position of the chair was different.

Her heart pounding, she tried to recall what it was that looked different. The vision eluded her, like a shadow scurrying ahead of a searchlight. She glanced at the chair. The eerie gray-green light, filtering through the window behind it, made a figure seem to sit there. Reassured, she closed her eyes.

Her sense of the room returned slowly. The walls felt close and somehow menacing. Furniture was not in the right places. The windows looked as if black paint had been sprayed over them, and only gradually did she realize that it was not paint but the inky darkness dimming their surfaces. The dark corner beside the stairwell contained something she could not bear to see. She told herself that no power must force her to look there. She looked at the man instead. Suddenly time seemed to spin dizzyingly. This was no longer the home she had meant to come to. It was no longer late afternoon, or today at all. It was late at night. She and the man were sitting up talking far into the night.

"If only you could cry," the voice said.

Meredith wanted to open her eyes. She wanted to check one last time to see that no one was there. She wanted to return to the home, to the life she had known. She could not move. A terrible laziness filled her, and she slowly came to know that it would not matter if she looked. The stranger was there and he was not there. He would wait for her until she went to him. He would wait.

He would always be waiting and she could not escape anything he intended to do.

"I can't cry." Her voice sounded weak and uncertain. It was not her own voice speaking, but a voice speaking through her lips.

The man took a deep breath. "It's what you need to do—cry. I only want to hold you. I won't hurt you. Can't you trust me?"

With cold shock, Meredith realized that to cry would be dangerous. If she cried, if one sliver of ice broke from the glacier, it would all tumble. If she cried he would come over to her. He would crouch behind the sofa and touch her, place his hands on her flesh and lean his head near to hers. He would hurt her. It would happen again, all over again. But it must not. She could not bear to be touched like that again.

The sofa stood by the wall, she reminded herself. He could not move behind it. Yet the vision said that he could, even if it was impossible.

"No!" The word came as a shout. "I'm not going to cry. That's what you want, isn't it? Then you would feel . . ." She stopped in horror. Searing emotional pain engulfed her. She had struck out at him. She did not want to hurt him. It was not his fault. Waves of shame and self-hatred washed over her.

A tremble began in her chest, but then, in the instant before it seemed the pain would pick her up and shake her in the air like a rag doll, it subsided. She felt as if she had escaped a furnace only to be plunged into a cold pool. Everything inside her grew still.

Exhausted, Meredith fell back against the sofa. She looked at the man. He had pushed himself abruptly from the chair, and now in three rapid strides, he reached the fireplace. He was farther away there and it felt safer. He turned on his heel and strode back, closer and more terrifying. As he walked, he moved through places where furniture ought to stand. The familiar library table and love seat were not there. He reached the armchair again—much too close—spun, and paced back toward the fireplace. She could see his face. Gray drapes were illuminated from outside as lightning crackled.

His brow was furrowed and the scar over his eyebrow had gone scarlet with anger. His hands, clenched in fists, swung like heavy steel weights at the ends of his arms. *He can hurt me,* Meredith thought. She tried to move, but the drowsy weight of helplessness held her down.

At last he came again to the chair and threw his weight into it. One hand shoved a wave of brown hair from his eyes. Tormented eyes glared at her. They were deep and penetrating. In their gray-blue recesses lay every emotion she knew—pain and anger, impatience and a desperate longing. He glared for a long moment before his chin fell in resignation. He stared at the dark carpet. He had not touched her, she realized. She was safe for now, yet she had no certainty of how long it would last.

"No one will hurt you while I'm here. You know that."

It was true. She felt grateful. He would protect her. He would keep violence away from her, would allow no one to tear at her clothes. He would hold her gently as he always had, and there would be no screams or fear, no blows or weight pressing her down. There would be only him. She could stand that if only he did not touch her.

"What about the child?" he said slowly. "You said you wanted a child. I want one, too, but we can't go on like this. We can't keep waiting. I need you. I want to touch you and hold you. I'm a man, can you understand that?" His head jerked up and that bright gaze pierced her again.

The depth of what he said dawned in Meredith's thoughts only slowly. She did want a child, she remembered. If only a baby were growing in her, if another life depended on her, this huge blanket of exhaustion would lift. The ice would melt. She would live again. She would be able to love.

"I want a baby," she said, and the effort of speaking made her throat ache. "I want that more than anything. I do."

"Then let me touch you."

He sounded too near. Meredith raised her eyes and saw that he had risen and taken a step, his right arm lifting. His hand drifted toward her, the fingers wide and sturdy, spreading as they moved through the air. Soon his hand would reach her. Its crushing weight would fall on her hair.

Meredith tried to speak, to cry out, but the words would not come. She opened her lips, willing her throat to scream, straining like a swimmer who could not quite reach the surface.

"No!"

The word burst out and Meredith's eyelids snapped open. She stared around, amazed at what she saw.

The room was dark, and yet she knew she could see it. Her hands felt rough wads of fabric, and her fingers ached. They gripped the edge of the sofa for what seemed an eternity after she willed them to let go. Then she lifted her hands toward her face, her fingers aching from the struggle to unlock. From the dark corner by the stairwell came muted echoes of struggle. Her own hands, the skin of her fingers, felt the pushing and tearing of that struggle. Something hideous lived beside that stairwell or was dying there.

Then she heard a sound. Two beams of light penetrated the darkness and swept through the room. They showed gray walls, and glanced over pale furniture and a shining row of books that should not have been on the mantel. The lights were headlights. A car turned into the drive. Richard.

Moments later, as she clung to the sink shaking, Meredith heard Richard's key enter the lock. She stood in the kitchen, unable to remember how she got here. She only knew she had run, stumbling and bumping into the doorway, struggling to get out of that awful gray room.

She glanced at the clock. It was quarter to six. Where had the afternoon gone?

She could remember parts of it, voices, a few words, a roaring torrent of emotion. She wondered how much of it could have been real. It had been like living someone else's life, a very bad life that tumbled over and over itself in helplessness.

"Hello, darling." Richard's familiar greeting coincided with the solid closing of the front door. "Dark in here. Anybody home?"

Meredith turned and forced herself to call back. Her hands still ached with the memory of fighting against whatever had held her, but she forced them open. She commanded them to slowly, calmly unwrap the steak she had set out earlier to defrost. "What smells so good?" Richard called, coming closer. "I smell fruit. Are you baking something?"

Meredith turned in time to see him enter the kitchen.

He smiled and stepped close to brush her cheek with a kiss. "What's cooking, fruit dessert?"

Meredith looked away. She pretended to be absorbed in slicing fat from the ragged edges of the steak. "Nothing. Actually, dinner's not, well, quite ready," she stammered. She tried to think how to go on, but he had stepped back to survey her figure.

"Stayed overtime in the clothing stores, I see. And bought a new dress."

"I did, but how did you know?" Meredith felt amazed. She watched as confusion clouded her husband's eyes.

"It's all right, I guess." Richard turned to walk back toward the living room. "Pretty. But I'm not sure it's quite you."

Her legs trembling, Meredith followed as far as the living room door. She stopped there. The walls were once more the pleasant coral color she had chosen for them three weeks ago. She looked down and stood stunned. She was wearing the brown nylon dress.

Chapter 6

The minute Meredith lifted her shovel, preparing to put up the yard sale sign, Elsa Johnson burst from the doorway of her house. Meredith heard her name called and set the shovel down, watching Elsa march up the block.

"There was another one," the large woman called as she came into hearing. "It happened again. Just as I expected."

"What happened? Another what?" Meredith resented the interruption. She had stopped to put up the yard sale sign while on the way to her car. She had no time to waste.

"Another *incident*. I heard it on the radio. And they almost caught the man. By the way, where are you off to so early?"

"An appointment," Meredith said, and added silently, *from which you are not going to keep me*. Gus Halburton's only free hour, as she had learned when she called first thing that morning, was between ten and eleven. She meant to take advantage of it. "And what happened? What was on the radio?"

"They say—mind you this was on the nine-thirty

news—the man was standing around the alley behind Economy Grocery. You know that one on Third? Well, now, according to the report, one of the high school girls took a shortcut, and what do you think happened?"

Meredith lifted the shovel and struck the soft turf. She pried up a piece of sod. "I think the man tried something illegal." She struggled to keep the annoyance from her voice. "He nearly got caught. You heard it on the radio."

Elsa pressed her lips tightly together and glared. "Well, if you know all that, what's the sense of my saying so? I mean, considering . . ."

"Considering what?" Meredith pushed the stick holding the sign into the soft soil. It held. She felt faintly sorry; she had not meant to hurt Elsa. On the other hand, no one had enough patience to always handle Elsa gently. "How does that look? And you said another incident? Did something happen before?"

Elsa cast a critical glance at the sign and shrugged. "Yes, something happened," she said coolly. "Something certainly *did* happen."

"I have a radio in my car," Meredith said. "No doubt I'll get a clearer picture."

"A high school girl," Elsa said. "Probably no better than she should be. Girls nowadays . . ." Elsa trailed off, but it was obvious she would not allow her story to be spoiled by a news report on a car radio. "Three times before," she said. "Three women. He wears a mask, like on Halloween. That's what I heard. He makes those women do things." Her lips pursed, and it was obvious to Meredith that Elsa could not bring herself to use the word *rape*.

So that was why women did not work in their yards alone. That was why children were kept close to the house. That was why men walked to the store, not women. What had she and Richard gotten into? This was a nice neighborhood. Things like this weren't supposed to happen. Meredith picked up the shovel and carried it to the garage. Anger and a touch of despair followed her. She had Richard, and she had a nice home. Now she felt attacked, not only from the stranger within her home, but from some unknown rapist outside. That, at least, explained the eerie feeling the other morning while painting the mailbox. The whole situation seemed to tarnish everything she and Richard had hoped for.

"I'd appreciate hearing more about it," she said over her shoulder to Elsa, "but let's save it for another day, can we? Want to come for coffee Wednesday?"

"Wednesday's my beauty-parlor day," Elsa said firmly.

"I forgot," Meredith lied. "Perhaps some other day. If I don't see you, be sure to come to the sale on Saturday."

She regretted being so abrupt, and she regretted it more when she saw Elsa's reaction. The woman knew she was being dismissed, and anger made her cheeks puff and her eyes seem smaller. "There's more than men doing illegal things around here," she said, and looked directly at Meredith's house. "There's been death around here. Very ugly. Very sad."

Meredith told herself that she really had to leave or be late for the appointment. She was shocked and, watching Elsa's eyes, believed that Elsa was lying. "I've heard no such thing," Meredith said. "You'll surely want to tell me about it."

The older woman did not reply. She had turned to watch a yellow compact car that turned the corner and now moved slowly up the block.

Meredith leaned the shovel against the garage door, picked up her handbag, and walked to her car. Maybe

when she started the engine, Elsa would give another
tidbit of information. If, that is, Elsa really did have any
information. Meredith pulled open the car's door and
was about to slide in when Elsa's voice stopped her.

"Well, can you believe that?" the older woman called
breathily. She watched the yellow car recede up the
block. "Of all the nerve."

"Believe what?" Meredith paused long enough to call
back.

"Oh nothing, nothing." Elsa slipped her hands into the
pockets of her housedress. "Just someone I thought I
knew. Have a good—where was it you said you were
going?"

"An appointment. And you have a good day, too."

Meredith eased into the car seat, started the motor, and
waited until Elsa stepped from the drive before backing
out. The woman was impossible, and now Meredith
believed that Elsa was also a liar. Elsa continued to stare
up the street, her head shaking from side to side.
Probably the yellow car would give her something else to
be mysterious about. Meredith pulled into the street,
thinking of noises at night, thinking of screams from the
darkness, thinking of the ache of the struggle from
Friday afternoon's illusion. She almost raced away from
her house, and from Elsa.

The sound of the old biddy's voice kept echoing in her
thoughts. She turned on the car radio to block it out.
Unfortunately, after a single song, the news came on. It
was Elsa all over again.

"A third brutal attack has been reported in the
Mabton-Westwood area," a chillingly calm male voice
announced. The report drew out the details—an unseen
assailant, a woman nearly strangled—before Meredith's
hand could reach the knob to spin it down the broadcast

band. She did not need this today. No one needed this, and today, especially now, her imagination resonated with that poor woman's terror. That woman, she knew at once, must feel it was all her fault. Meredith wasn't sure how she knew this, but she did. At last the tuner caught the sound of violin strings. That felt better. It was safe music. More than anything, the frightened part of her mind, a part that apparently grew more vivid on some days, wanted to be safe. Meredith had always disliked the sound of Mantovani strings, but today his songs comforted her all the way to the college.

Twenty minutes later, settled into a burgundy armchair outside the door marked Chairman—Department of Psychology, Meredith dismissed the echoes of problems from her mind. She had only ten minutes to make a decision, and thinking of terror or even watching the psychology department's head secretary type efficiently at her desk nearby was not going to help. She had to decide what to tell Gus. There was no sense going in and spilling the whole story. After all, this ridiculous business probably added up to nothing.

The dreams had not returned over the weekend. Friday afternoon's session had either done the trick or, as she had begun to suspect this morning, merely yanked the problem from the world of dreams into the more real and frightening realm of waking hallucination. She would not have thought so on Saturday or Sunday. Now the suspicion nibbled at her peace of mind.

She and Richard spent Saturday raking the leaves that the storm had scattered over the yard. Sunday morning was taken up with reading papers, and in the afternoon they worked together to prepare an elaborate three-course meal. They ate it all by themselves by candlelight, delighting in their selfishness. No question, the weekend had gone perfectly. It was only this morning, and then only briefly, that Meredith began to suspect she was not yet free of the stranger.

The moment Richard's car pulled from the drive and the sound of its engine faded with distance, a pall seemed to settle over the house. Meredith tried to busy herself with the breakfast dishes. She worked at the sink, but felt a presence, an air of hollow expectancy, gathering at her back. She turned more than once to check over her shoulder. The kitchen looked as it always had. Nothing there.

Nevertheless, the hint of a presence persisted. It hovered near while she called the university, then followed upstairs to wait politely while she dressed and put on her makeup, a devoted servant marking time outside the bedroom door. She glanced out the door once, unable to restrain herself. No one stood there; only the hallway carpet, vacuumed this morning, stretched smooth and unruffled toward the staircase. Except in one spot. She looked closer. Two shoe-sized shapes, too large to be her own, flattened the weave directly outside the bedroom door. Meredith shook her head, chasing off the scare. These shapes did not flatten the carpet very much. Richard must have stood there. Then she'd missed that spot when she vacuumed.

Meredith returned to the bedroom to finish dressing, and collected her bag and jacket, determined to ignore the illusion, this imaginary friend her mind had invented. Not until she pulled the front door shut and stepped out on the porch did the aura diminish. It was uncanny. For two hours she felt sure another person was sharing the house. Most peculiar of all, while the presence felt frightening, somewhere deeper it whispered a promise of security.

Meredith heard a buzzing sound and looked up. The psychology department's secretary clicked off her typewriter, answered the phone, then glanced toward Meredith. "You may go in now." She laid the receiver down. "The doctor will see you."

Meredith stood, annoyed at being mistaken for a patient. Not that there was anything wrong with needing help, as long as you were not patronized. In a way, she did need help. Perhaps it was just as well she had not decided how much to tell Halburton. As the office door swung open, she knew Gus would probably get the whole truth despite her intentions.

Chapter 7

Gus Halburton looked as welcoming and bearlike as she had hoped. He stepped from behind his broad desk and hurried across the office to meet her halfway. His arms spread wide, closing her in a hug against the rough tweed of his coat. She smelled wool and pipe smoke. His warmth and strength engulfed her until he stepped back, hands firm on her shoulders.

"Meredith, dear lady," he said as if that were statement enough. "To think you've been in town a month. And I've been gallivanting off to worthless conferences."

"Gus, you look wonderful."

He certainly did. Wide brown eyes sparkled above his ruddy cheeks. The salt-and-pepper gray hair she remembered was sprinkled more liberally with salt, but the new lines in his face were in all the right places, betraying seven years of smiles rather than worries.

"And you grew a beard," she added with surprise.

Gus released one shoulder to tug at the curls lining his jaw. "At my age, you hide as much as you can." He chuckled. "Best to leave the secrets of age to the imagination."

Meredith exaggerated her frown.

"But look at you," he hurried on. "It's you I want to hear about. And Richard, and your new house. All morning I've been looking forward to this good news."

Gus hustled a leather chair closer to the desk and fussed like a mother hen until she was seated comfortably and the office door was closed. Then he eased into his own chair, somewhat more gingerly than years ago, and took his pipe from the ashtray. He leaned back.

"We can skip most of the case history," he joked in mock professional tones. "All that boring business about toilet training and early childhood. Go straight to recent history. What brings my favorite couple to Mabton?"

"Work." Meredith spread her palms open and shrugged. "And a lot more. It all happened so fast, I hardly know where to begin. You remember Richard joined that small family firm years ago?"

Gus nodded.

"Well, we liked it there. You saw the town, and my practice was going wonderfully. But Richard wanted more challenge." Meredith hurriedly outlined the events leading up to the offer from Mabton. The words came easily, and for the first time in weeks she felt at ease. While she talked she took in the rich familiarity of her surroundings.

This new office was larger than Halburton's old one. Shelves of books lined the walls, and many of their bindings were familiar, but the new spines beside them tantalized her interest with their titles. A red Oriental rug with an intriguing pattern covered the floor, and soft light spread from two antique lamps, one near the desk and a second beside the wide oak door.

The broad mahogany desk was the one she remembered, and while the arms of his favorite leather chair showed the years of wear, the chair itself fit in perfectly with its new surroundings. On the walls, beside his treasured collection of children's artwork, hung even more gold-lettered certificates. Over the years she had followed Halburton's growing reputation in professional journals, and Meredith felt glad he was at last receiving the recognition he deserved.

A gallery of photographs filled the windowsill. She recognized the faces of former students and, set apart from these, to one side, the gold frames holding pictures of Gus's children and his wife. He had been married to her for many years before she died a decade ago. Gus had told Meredith privately that he did not expect to meet so fine a woman ever again.

Gus himself showed the passage of years only slightly. His movements, when he occasionally shifted in the chair, were somewhat slower, but his smile was quick and his gaze clear and steady. He fiddled with the briarwood pipe, using a brass tool to dig ashes, then tamp new tobacco. He allowed the pipe to roll sideways in his grasp as if he had forgotten to light it.

Meredith spoke freely and easily, as she always had with Gus. She described their move and Richard's new duties as project manager.

"He loves the work. Besides, I'm absolutely delighted with the house we found." Her voice faltered for the first time in the narrative, but she hurried on. They were completely moved in, she added, and she was thinking of setting up a new practice.

"But first, before anything, I must have you to dinner." She paused, suddenly aware that she had been doing all the talking. "Oh, I go on and on. I've probably bored you to tears." She wondered if she sounded as phony as she felt.

"You could never bore me." Gus lifted his pipe again.

He studied the tobacco tucked in its bowl, his expression faintly perplexed. "Now, I could bore you, telling what it's like to be head of a department. And suffering with that ogre of a secretary I inherited."

He gestured toward the office door and gave a wink. Then, as if his smile slipped behind a cloud, his face became thoughtful. "It's you I want to hear about, though. I know all about Richard now, and the job, and the house. I even know your nosiest neighbor on a first-name basis. But what about you? Let me think, any children?"

Meredith glanced away. "Not yet. Not exactly. I mean, we're thinking about it," she finished lamely. She tried to recover with a smile, but Gus had lowered his gaze. It was kindness, she realized. He would not stare at her while she was fumbling.

"So tell me," he said at last, "how is my Meredith? I've got the frame, the canvas, and a wall to hang it on. All I need now is a picture."

Meredith smiled. It was an old joke between them. Patients invariably talked first about everything but the problem. Meredith exhaled a deep sigh of admiration. Gus always knew.

She tried to decide where to begin. Seven years had passed, but that was not the difficulty. She felt more like a college girl, seated in the safety of his office, ready to pour out her grief over statistical analysis. Only today's fear was a whole lot deeper than a computer printout. She felt stupid for believing that Gus could untangle it as easily.

She searched for the best words, something not too near the truth, but not a willful deception, either. The words did not come. At last she gave up and asked for help.

"You tell me?" She risked a glance at his wide, inquiring brown eyes. "I mean what do you see? You probably already know more than I could tell you."

"What do I see?" A gentle smile flickered over the large man's features. He selected a match from the tray on his pipe stand, struck it on a strip of flint, and held the flame close to his pipe. When he had drawn the fire down and rich clouds of smoke billowed, he slowly waved the match out.

"I see a beautiful woman. I see my brightest student who has fulfilled every hope I had for her, and still has time and energy for more. I see promise. I see sparkle and loveliness. And beyond that, I see something else." He paused, taking a long pull on the pipe. He let the smoke rise.

"Beyond that, because you ask me honestly, I see fear. You are anxious, Meredith. Something is making you afraid. I don't think it's wrong for me to ask what it is."

Meredith lowered her gaze. Her hands gripped each other so tightly in her lap that the knuckles stood out bright white. She waited to be sure Gus had finished, then spoke without looking up.

"That's true, I mean about the house, the job. We really are happy," she said at last. "But you're right. This other thing, this 'something else' as you call it, it's aside from the happiness. It's not in the daylight, Gus. It's in the night."

She looked up. Gus was nodding slowly, his steady gaze an assurance that nothing she could say would offend him. She went on.

"I have frightening dreams. For a while they came almost every night. They're all about the same man. I don't know who he is, and in the dreams, even out of them now, I feel afraid. You said I look frightened. I am," she finished.

"Perhaps you could tell me when they began," Gus said softly. "I want to know everything you want to tell me."

"At first I thought he was someone I'd seen." Meredith recounted her theory about an encounter at Westwood. As she described the dreams, how they placed her at a cocktail party or in a park where she had never been, she could feel the warmth in the older man's attentive silence. She told how the stranger's presence had gradually crept into her awareness. Then it had pressed closer and closer until now she not only knew what he looked like but recognized his voice.

"You tried doing dream enactment?" Gus put in, not so much to prompt as to assure her that every word was being heard.

"I did. And, well, it was terrifying. It got worse."

She told of Friday afternoon's bizarre sequence of events, how she had progressed from disbelief, pretending to a vision, to full-blown hallucination. Halburton's steady gaze never left her face, except to glance away once or twice to where her hands twisted in her lap.

"It was so awful," she said at last. "I almost believed he was really there. And then to have changed clothes, for no reason. And not to remember." She shuddered and looked up. "I think I understand what patients mean now. When they say they feel they're going crazy."

Meredith stopped speaking. She let go of a long, painful breath. Slowly the knot her fingers had formed began to unwind. The burden of the past weeks lay between them now, an ominous-looking package still unopened on the desk. It belonged to both of them, she realized. She was not alone anymore.

Gus had let his pipe burn out. He stared down at it, but seemed unaware. Then he let his glance drift upward, watching a thought that only he could see rising in the air.

Meredith waited, tension ebbing from her chest. At last Gus leaned forward to brace his elbows on the green blotter.

"The man really was there," he said firmly. "For the mind, it does not matter if something exists in three dimensions. The mind is wiser than we are, Meredith. It shows us things not because they merely exist, but because we need to see them. The question, as always, is why? In your case, there are several possible explanations. You've explored two." He paused and cast an inquiring glance at her.

Meredith nodded.

"I can think of two other explanations," Halburton continued. "But before I talk, you must answer the most important question. Do you feel—please be honest with me—do you feel that you're ready to hear and possibly reject another analysis?"

"I certainly need one." Meredith smiled. It was the first genuine and easy smile she had felt since coming here. "If it's not your opinion that I'm going crazy. If that's your answer, I don't want to hear it."

Laughing, Gus leaned back in his chair. "No, my dear, you are not crazy. The word means nothing, and even if it did, you're a poor candidate for the asylum. You know too much about yourself, not too little. And that's why I agree, for the most part, with your own best analysis. You misunderstood the signals, that's all. Like all young people, you look for an answer that is easiest to find."

The stranger did not have to be anyone she had seen,

Gus explained gently. She might have created a composite of many men, but the reason for her creation was what mattered. No question about it, she was lonely. She had left family, friends, and clients behind and come to a new place. Richard was at work all day. Even when he was home, he would be tired and distracted by his new duties. Of course she was lonely. As for Friday's events, they were frightening, he agreed, but the mind's logic hid behind them like a mischievous imp.

"When people move, not only do their surroundings change, Meredith, they change, too. Buying a new dress, putting it on without thinking, these things could be read as symbols. A world rich in possibility has opened for you. You must discover who you want to become in this new setting."

Halburton continued, his explanation sure and knowledgeable. Meredith let the comfort of his words soothe her. Each thing he said added another piece of the puzzle. At last she felt the weight of the dreams lift.

"And this morning? When I thought someone else was in the house?"

Gus raised his bushy eyebrows and gave a slight smile.

"I was alone again," she answered her own question. "Richard left for work and there I was. No one to be with. Nothing to do."

Gus spread his hands palms down on the green blotter. "Exactly. But only if we want to accept this answer. Remember, no one said that we have to."

Gus turned his attention to the task of relighting his pipe, waiting while Meredith tried the explanation on for size. She matched it to her own feelings. The explanation fit. It accounted for the insignificant, frightened woman she became in the dreams and for the unreal lapses into dreamlike wakefulness that had come over her lately. A need did lie unsatisfied in her. It was a need to be known and recognized, something more than a faceless housewife falling prey to her buttinsky neighbor. But what about the helpless compulsion to buy the brown dress, she wondered suddenly. And what about those two footprints on the hallway rug? She was sure she had vacuumed carefully.

Maybe she had not. Of course they were Richard's prints. Loneliness, wishful thinking for company; either one had to be the right explanation.

It was the explanation she had seen first, but she had not looked deeply enough into the loneliness. To be absolutely certain, she asked, "So I have to unpack my life here as well? Redecorate my world with new friends and new activities?"

"That would be my first recommendation for therapy." Gus leaned forward again. "You must create a new world. Or your mind will do the job for you, as we have seen. You must find out who you are in this new world. The mind is so susceptible to change, Meredith." He smiled and gave a rueful laugh. "Look at me. I get a promotion. They give me a fancy office and a high-priced secretary, and what do I do? Grow a beard. I get all grizzled to confirm my old homeliness."

Gus extended his arms over the desk. Meredith lifted her own hands into his and felt them warmly squeezed.

"I get out to meet the neighbors this Saturday," she assured him. "At least I hope they come. I've giving a sale."

"Good. And if they don't come, you'll think of something else. Give a party. Join a club. Or set up practice so I have someone I trust to send the worst cases to."

Meredith laughed. She had not been so at ease in a long time. This explanation had to be true. She gave his hands a quick squeeze and let them go. "And I'll bother you for advice on what to do for them."

She smoothed her dress on her lap, stood, and pushed back the heavy chair. She had taken more than her hour already, she should go. Nevertheless, a shadow of doubt lingered. She could not resist the impulse to settle it.

"You said you had a couple of explanations. What was the second? If I'm not going crazy, that is."

Using the sides of his chair, Gus pushed himself to his feet, then walked to the side of his desk. He closed his arm around her shoulder to guide her toward the door. "Pooh, that. You see those?" He gestured toward the stack of papers and books that covered the top of an antique table.

"That's this week's reading from last week's conference. And I must somehow read it with a straight face and a serious frame of mind. I went to the conference strictly, strictly," he emphasized, "because the college president demanded I go. He gets excited about all the new stuff. They called the conference the Interim Review of Parapsychology and Unexplained Phenomenan. I call it hooey. At least I called it that to the college president's face before I left." He paused and looked thoughtful. "Some of the papers were surprisingly well documented. Interesting ideas."

"And your second explanation?" Meredith glanced from the pile of papers and books to his face.

"Their explanation, not mine. I'm not ready for spirits and talking tables. Perfectly rational men were there who would have said you were experiencing a visitation—maybe a poltergeist—although I don't think so." Gus waved a hand in a vague way. "They have all kinds of classifications. A lost spirit needs fulfillment or revenge or both—or a better brand of mortuary clothing, I presume. Check with me after I do the reading, will you? I might know more by then, or I'll tell you all about it by ESP."

Meredith took hold of the doorknob, laughing. "You'll tell us all about it on Thursday," she insisted. "It will make wonderful dinner-table discussion."

"Deal," Gus agreed. Then he hesitated. "But don't worry, dear. Not a word about the dreams to your husband. Poor fellow."

The secretary in the outer office was on her feet before the door swung completely open.

"Dr. Halburton." She glared at Meredith. "You are seven minutes late for Faculty Forum."

"Ah me," Gus said, sighing. "I'll have to retire before they give me the watch that keeps my kind of time."

Chapter 8

Meredith emerged from the plate-glass doorway of the new psychology building to the splendor of an early-autumn day. A lace of clouds fringed the horizon, but the sky overhead was as royal blue as a china bowl. The carefully pruned trees that lined the campus walkways were losing leaves, and a few completely bare branches laid herringbone patterns against the sky. On the green lawns, fallen leaves overlapped and drifted in the light breeze; a rippling, crazy quilt of red, yellow, and orange.

On the walkways, where students laden with books hurried between classes, footsteps had ground the fallen leaves to a fine texture like oatmeal. It puffed upward and scurried ahead of her steps. The students were colorfully dressed, wearing bright plaid jackets and knitted caps, maroon-and-gold collegiate sweaters, and bearing the obligatory green or blue book bags on their shoulders.

Meredith decided to join them. She had no reason to hurry. She would spend the afternoon among the familiar sights and sounds of the campus, visiting old haunts and discovering the many new buildings. Gus had said she needed to re-create her identity. There seemed no better way than to review memories of a place she had once thought of as home.

She decided to go to the library first. On its steps, one similar afternoon eight years ago, she had accidentally and on purpose stumbled and dropped an arm load of books at the feet of a handsome student. Richard's boyish charm when he stooped on hands and knees to pick them up had confirmed her attraction.

Meredith pulled back the wrought-iron handle of the heavy door and inhaled the faintly musty smell of books and papers that was inseparable from her memory of college. She hurried at once to where the psychology collection had been kept, but found it had been moved. She followed a labyrinth of corridors and call numbers to the new location. From the rows and rows of shelves there, she selected a handful of books with the newest bindings. These she lugged upstairs to a study desk beneath the arched Gothic ceiling of the graduate reading room and settled down to skim their contents.

When she looked up an hour and a half later, the shafts of sunlight penetrating the stained glass along one wall had shifted positions. There were so many other places to see. She left the last book lying open on the desk, collected her handbag, and hurried down the worn stone stairs to discover that the day outside had only improved in its brilliance.

Her next stop, she determined, should be the old psychology building. It lay at the north end of campus, a small red brick structure that its namesake department had long since outgrown. It was devoted to laboratories and offices now, and as she toured its antiquated hallways she tried to recall where her classrooms had been, what courses she had studied in them, and the air of excitement fall semester always carried.

She remembered the graduate students' lounge on the top floor and climbed the stairs to stand outside its frosted-glass doors. A small card designated the hours it was open and posted flyers announced events that were scheduled, but midafternoon nostalgia was not listed among them. As she was about to turn back toward the stairs, a memory tugged at her.

It had something to do with what Gus had said. She searched her mind to recover the scene. Once, one of the other students had asked Meredith and several companions to be part of an experiment in telepathy. They had gathered in the lounge, exchanging flirtatious jokes about ESP and sexual attraction. Then they had settled down to work hard for the experimenter who needed the research to complete his work for a class.

Meredith was a Receptive. That was what the older student had said. She had passed all his tests with flying colors and so outperformed the others on the card-identification exercise that only their teasing masked open jealousy. A Receptive, according to the older student, was a person uniquely aware of unspoken thoughts. She would be an excellent subject for telepathy testing and was probably equally sensitive to messages from other worlds.

Meredith had laughed at the time, and she smiled at the memory now. She stepped lightly on her way down the staircase. Spirits and talking tables, Gus had called such work. Halburton's opinion was good enough for her.

A haze had gathered by the time she stepped outside again. The sun was moving toward the horizon, but she could not resist crossing the campus diagonally to make one last stop. The later she got home, it seemed, the better. She no longer felt afraid, Meredith reassured herself, but if she could avoid it, there was no point in spending even an hour alone in that empty house.

On the west side of campus the student union building that housed the cafeteria had been remodeled, but the dining room itself looked unchanged. The long wooden counters were scarred with a few more years' graffiti, but the middle-aged food service women with thick hair nets and big aprons appeared, almost miraculously, to be the same.

Meredith selected a root beer float from the cooler and threaded her way through the crowd of students to a table that offered the best view. She listened to the murmur of conversations about course work and midterm exams, then decided to test her powers of recall by cataloging the various types of students.

The engineering majors, who used to carry slide rules, now carried electronic calculators. The future scientists wore heavy rings at their hips filled with the many keys needed for opening laboratory doors and cabinets. Physical education majors passed in sweatshirts and jogging pants, while the literature students could be sorted into two groups: scruffy mop heads in blue jeans, and prim, pencil-thin fellows in gray V-necked sweaters, their conservative striped ties knotted hard against their Adam's apple.

Suddenly Meredith caught herself. For the last few minutes she had been watching only the men. For an instant she credited force of habit, left from college days, but then a pang of guilt cut into her. She knew what man she was looking for.

It was the stranger she wished to see. With a mixture of both dread and longing, she had searched the kaleidoscope of faces, seeking only his. She sat momentarily shocked. Here, so far from home, the stranger still intruded into her thoughts. Here, in this safe place, he could still make himself present in her mind.

Meredith stood and pulled her jacket over her shoulders. The stranger was not here, she told herself. He was not at home, not anywhere. It was time to get home, arriving, if necessary, before Richard got there. This evening she would have the pleasure of sharing news of changes at the college, and, more than that, extending her own renewed sense of well-being to Richard.

Several hours later, as she sat enjoying a cup of coffee after dinner, Meredith began to appreciate exactly how much her tour of the campus had meant. Over dinner she had described the easier portions of her meeting with Gus, and told Richard briefly about the high points of her afternoon walk. Now, although she felt slightly deceptive about the way she must go about it, she tried to explain what she had learned.

"Gus and I got talking," she began. "You know, not just about the move and old times, but about feelings."

Richard had untied his shoes and wriggled his feet out of them. He flexed his toes before raising his legs to rest his heels on the hassock in front of the yellow chair.

Over the weekend, Meredith had left the chair in its new position, in the exact spot where Friday's vision said it belonged. It still felt right in that place. Stretched comfortably in it, Richard's lanky frame looked tired but relaxed.

"You got to talking about feelings," he repeated her words. "Anything I should know?"

"A few." Meredith picked her way carefully, as if threading steps along the edge of a cliff. "I guess you and I haven't talked much about hopes and fears and all that lately."

Richard cocked his head sideways in concern. "I know," he said thoughtfully. "I've been missing it."

"So have I." Meredith paused, selecting a safe approach. It felt pleasant sitting with Richard, as comforting as if it were a memory of many shared evenings like this. She went on. "Gus said something about how when we move to a new town, we need to shape new personalities. Walking around campus today, I felt like myself again. I was whole, I was someone. I belonged in a place and it was wonderful."

Richard paused, considering her words. At last he spoke. "I know what you mean. Maybe I'm pushing it, but, well, that's why I thought about a baby." His voice trailed off uncertainly. He began again. "I mean if we put down roots, began planning and fixing up that empty room upstairs, wouldn't it be more like we were really here?"

A flicker of fear leaped into Meredith's chest. She glanced at the windows. They were black with night, but this was not that other conversation. Richard sat across from her, his gaze loving and tolerant. He was not that other man. The feeling was only an echo.

"Yes," she replied after a moment's hesitation. "It would be more like that."

The stranger was not here, she told herself. She had left the stranger in Halburton's office, or at least left him in the college cafeteria, and the whole business was over. He did not seem even remotely present during the half hour after she had come home and before Richard arrived.

Nevertheless, it felt too soon to answer Richard's question. She wanted everything to be right before she made that decision.

Richard was waiting, his calm gaze fixed on her.

"I do want children," she managed at last. "But right now, it's so final. It's a decision that will change our whole life. I go this way, then that way. I want it. I just can't seem to take the step."

She thought of the small pastel purse containing her diaphragm tucked away upstairs in the drawer of her nightstand. If only she could forget to reach for it once, the decision might be made.

"We could decide by indifference." Richard's eyebrows lifted quizzically.

"Meaning?"

"Meaning, come on over here." Richard patted his thigh. "Have a seat on my lap, little girl. I'll teach you all about indifference."

Meredith laughed. She watched as Richard's most charming and salacious smile spread over his face. Then she stood and stepped around the coffee table. His strong hands grabbed her arms and pulled her down on his lap.

"For your first lesson in indifference, pay no attention to what my hands might do," he said, nuzzling her neck.

Meredith felt the warmth of his touch begin to arouse her. A shadow of doubt crossed her mind, but she pushed it away. They did want a child and the stranger was gone. She let her emotions carry her along and closed her arms around Richard's firm back to squeeze him close. Then she was jolted alert.

The phone rang. It brrrr-inged again, a shrill stab into the moment.

"Damn," Richard breathed against her neck. "Can we ignore that?"

"Better not." Meredith extracted herself from his arms and hurried toward the kitchen. Since they had not yet made friends, hardly anyone called. It might be long distance from one of their families. That would mean trouble.

Meredith laid her hand on the receiver and paused to catch her breath. She was trembling and a chill passed over her, a shudder of premonition and dread. She felt afraid to pick it up. What was wrong with her these days?

"Have you got it?" Richard called as the bell rang once more.

Meredith steeled herself and pressed the receiver to her ear.

"Hello, Mrs. Morgan?"

"Yes?" Meredith's breath came in short, shallow gasps. The voice sounded faintly familiar. She thought of the boy at the hardware store. It was too deep for his voice.

"I'm sorry to disturb you," a man stammered. His voice sounded thick, as if he might have been drinking. "I hope you don't mind my calling. Excuse me, you don't know my name. I'm Arthur Watson and I, I happened to pass your house today. I saw a sign in the yard."

"Yes," Meredith answered, filling the man's embarrassed silence. She felt sorry for him, whoever he was. He seemed overcome with shame at calling strangers unexpectedly. A thought struck her. "But how did you get our number?"

"Oh, information, new listings. Well, really, I saw your name on the mailbox and just figured. I mean I hope I'm not too rude."

"Of course not," she reassured him. "What did you call about?"

Richard had come out to stand beside her, leaning seductively in the kitchen doorway. He lifted his hand,

and one finger drew a light, enticing line along her neck.

Meredith covered the receiver. Squinching up her face, she hissed, "Don't distract me," then spoke into the receiver again. "Yes, go on."

Arthur Watson explained that he had recently moved. He was about to move again. His company was sending him to Europe, and he had a few things he wanted to sell but no time to do it himself. Would she be willing to include them as part of her sale?

"I'd be glad to," Meredith assured him hastily. She would have agreed to housebreak his pet Saint Bernard if it would get her off the phone. Richard's fingers had renewed their feather-light teasing, and she had difficulty concentrating on the man's stammered words.

"You could keep the proceeds," the man rushed ahead. Then he corrected himself. "No, that doesn't make sense, does it? I mean, since I want to sell them. I mean, keep part of the proceeds, of course."

"That would be fine," Meredith answered firmly. "I'll be home Friday morning, you could drop them by. Is there much?"

"No, I didn't keep much." The man paused. "That is, when I moved. Your yard sale just seemed like a good . . . a good place." He took a deep breath and when he spoke again the depth had returned to his voice. "Thank you very much, Mrs. Morgan."

Meredith hung up and quickly explained what the man had called about. His last words echoed in her thoughts, bringing an uncomfortable chill. She could have sworn she had heard him speak before, or heard someone who had a voice like his. She felt that in only a moment the voice would connect with a face. She would know who he was.

"Don't say another word." Richard's arms encircled

her from behind. "You're coming upstairs. There's no time to waste on this baby-making project."

"What?" she said, laughing, pretending to struggle as he successfully marched her toward the living room. She halfheartedly clung to the living room doorjamb, making him pull her free. "You said we had all the time in the world. We'd be together forever."

"That was before. I'm going out of town next Monday. Got to get you pregnant before I go sterile from airport X rays."

Meredith laughed, clinging unsteadily to the banister. He half dragged, half carried her up the steps. The heel of her shoe caught on the rug and she felt the shoe slip free to tumble down the stairs.

All at once, with the sound of the shoe falling, a wall of coldness washed over her skin. She lurched against the banister, her mind suddenly woozy. The echo of a scream came from the dark corner beside the stairwell. Meredith fought the cold and the echo, but they were too sheer and dark, flowing through her flesh. The shoe clunk-clunk-clunked down three more steps before settling to a stop. Meredith fought the rush of air speeding past her skin as she felt that she was falling with it, like a death wind as she dropped down the stairwell herself into darkness.

Richard still tugged at her arm, and she pulled herself away from the dragging of darkness, the force wanting to pull her down. She felt that she was nearly staggering as she entered the bedroom and lay on the bed. Beyond the bedroom door, down in that hollow of darkness, voices sobbed, claimed they loved, and sobbed and sobbed.

Richard heaved a mock sigh, then chuckled. She lay shaking, struggling to cover the awful shivering that gripped her, trying to make it look as though these were gusts of laughter making her tremble on the bed. Richard must not know. He must not realize how near the well of darkness had come.

Above her, Richard unbuckled his belt. He whipped it free of its loops.

A memory tugged at her. She wanted only a few moments to review the sound of that voice on the phone. There was something in it that stirred the memory and brought the blackness. It was a voice that seemed intimate.

There was no time now. Richard's weight eased onto the bed. This could not be the man's voice, she told herself. She was imagining that. This endless well, this sense of darkness could not truly come from memory. She had searched every face in the cafeteria today for a hint of the stranger. Now she was imagining his voice, too.

Strong hands gripped her shoulders. Richard's silhouette rose over her, a black cutout in the dim light from the hallway.

"It's only fair to ask," he said softly, his voice empty of laughter. "Will it be love on the half shell, or not?"

Despite the fond reference to her diaphragm, Meredith read the seriousness in his words. She thought a moment, then, without a word, rolled onto her stomach. She stretched to reach the nightstand drawer, and her fingers located her diaphragm.

"I'm sorry," she said to Richard's waiting silence. "I have some things to think through. Soon. I promise, I'll be sure."

Chapter 9

In her dream they lay side by side on a golden beach. The sun was hot, intensified by reflections off the sand and the water. Meredith had one arm thrown over her eyes, and through her eyelashes she could see the water sparkling. Cries came from where children were playing at the edge of the water. The children were shadows flitting beneath a brilliant sun.

She could not see the man but she knew he lay beside her. Her right arm was outstretched and lying limp, supported by his chest. Her arm rose and fell with the gentle rhythm of his breathing.

Meredith did not know how long they had been lying here. She wished it could always be like this, but she knew it probably would not. Darkness or some danger would come. Something would change and she would lose him.

A shadow dimmed the sparkling light. He had stopped stroking her arm and moved to lean over her. Meredith pulled her hand back and looked up. His eyes were gray-green and they seemed oceans deep; momentarily inscrutable.

"You're awake," he said, his lips curling slightly in amusement. "I thought you must be sleeping."

Meredith did not speak. She let her gaze travel over his face, from the tousled light brown curls above his smooth tan forehead, over the finely chiseled nose and high cheekbones, then downward to his delicate, thin lips. She felt ephemeral, like a spirit that existed only through him.

With a vague sense of unease, Meredith remembered that she had, in some very different time, felt afraid of this man. A part of her wanted to laugh at that thought. She loved him. She had never wanted to be near anyone else. She could never fear him, not now, not ever in the future, no matter what happened.

"If we stay out much longer you'll get burned. It's your own fault for being blond."

The amusing comment struck Meredith as odd. She wanted to remind him that she was not blond, that her hair was much darker than his. His hand settled onto her thigh, the palm warm and smooth, fingers closing with a gentle hint of ownership.

That was why he wanted to go inside, Meredith realized, the realization coming from what seemed like the depth of someone else's memory. They had only a few more hours of afternoon left before they must leave and drive somewhere. If they went inside, they would make love, saying good-bye to the room the same way it had welcomed them. She wanted it, too. Yet it felt wrong for her to say so.

"Don't you think you'll get burned?" he said over his shoulder. The hand on her thigh moved. Meredith wished she could find words that were clever and sexy. She could make a joke, the way girls in the movies boldly teased men.

But she was not bold. She could never think of the

right words. He deserved someone better than a wallflower, though for some reason he had chosen her.

He had selected her because he loved her, she reminded herself. She did not know why. And now he had given her an opening to say she wanted to go to the room. He knew she was shy.

"I must be already red," she said at last. She immediately regretted the words.

"Red like a tomato," he laughed, "but I don't think it's all sunburn." He pushed himself to his feet and reached down to take her hands. He pulled her up. "Let me take you inside and put some lotion on that burn."

Meredith could not resist the smile breaking over her face. "Is that all?" she asked, looking up at him from under her lashes as the shadows of children flashed in the sun.

"No, that's not all," he said with a laugh. His arm encircled her waist to steady their steps over the sand. "I just didn't want to make you blush again."

The white walls of the lodge stood out ahead of them, its majesty accented by a crisscross pattern of pale blue tiles. On the patio at the side, young men and women sat at glass tables drinking from tall pastel glasses. They wore bright summer outfits, like actors in a luxurious movie scene. Meredith wished she could wear colors that bright. They looked pretty on other people, but when she wore them it seemed that everyone stared at her. She tugged her beach coat closed as they stepped onto the porch.

"I'll stop by the desk for a minute," he said, holding the door for her. "You go ahead up."

Meredith felt his presence drift away, his steps fading quickly on the soft carpet. She felt alone again, small and out of place in the immense lobby. It was more grand

than anything she had ever seen, wide and high and
ornate like the sky. He wanted them to have this, he had
said. These were the first days of their life together.

All of which meant she belonged here, Meredith told
herself. This hotel was hers for a few more hours. She
ran her hand along the smooth wood of the banister and
stepped on the first stair. For an instant she felt tall and
graceful, like a woman gliding up a staircase in a film.
She wished she could think of some bold and delightful
way to surprise him when he returned to the room. If
only he could walk in the door and find her waiting,
lying with nothing on, stretched out on top of the white
bedspread.

But she could not do it. She could think of so many
things, except she never could do them. When he
discovered that, when they had been together for awhile
and he became bored, that was when he would leave.

The hallway at the top of the stairs was brightly lit,
with a rich blue rug lining the floor. It looked lonely and
empty. He was not behind her. Maybe he was already
gone. Maybe she had already lost him. Meredith reached
a door at the end of the hall and slipped her key into the
lock. She heard shower water running and steam billowed as she opened the door.

That should not be, she thought. He was still down in
the lobby, settling the bill. She tried to see the room, but
steam from the shower filled it and made everything
fade. The steam pressed on her skin, a warm fuzziness.
She lifted her hand to brush it back from her eyes. Her
arm fell away against the pillow and hit the head of the
bed.

Meredith's eyelids fluttered open. The dream was
interrupted. She was in her own house. From somewhere

nearby she heard a swishing sound, and a haze of steam hung in the air. Richard had awakened early and was taking his shower.

Meredith jerked herself to a sitting position and glanced at the clock. Full daylight poured in the window. The dial on the clock said the alarm had already rung.

She threw back the covers, then fumbled beneath them to find her bathrobe. There had been a dream, she remembered. It had been a dream in which someone else seemed to be living her life, or she was living someone else's life. Bizarre. Richard's towel-wrapped figure emerged from the open bathroom door.

"Morning, sleepyhead." He grinned, toweling his hair. "Thought you were going to sleep all day."

"You're up early. Why didn't you leave the alarm on to wake me?"

"Are you kidding? You slept right through it." Richard let the towel drop over a chair and began pulling on his T-shirt.

Meredith watched him dress, this body that was so dear to her. They had made love last night. Then the dream happened. She never overslept, yet even now her body longed to lie down again. She remembered a portion of the dream. It was sweet and succulent, promising knowledge of another man's body. She wished she could return to that world, and then she felt both silly and disloyal.

"Just sleepy," she told Richard. She pushed herself to her feet. "If you're going to get any breakfast, I'd better hustle."

Richard was buttoning his shirt. "I don't even get a good-morning hug?"

Meredith crossed the room and lifted her arms to encircle his broad shoulders. He wanted her to hug him.

Why did that suddenly make her feel shy? On her cheek, the soft fabric of his shirt felt comforting. His grasp closed securely at her back, and she smelled the freshness of laundry soap mixed with the fragrance of shampoo.

"That's better." He gave a final squeeze before letting go.

"A minute longer," she whispered, and then held on, wishing she could explain. Just touching Richard made her feel more real.

An hour later, after her third cup of strong coffee, Meredith firmly and finally banished the dream from her mind. Richard's car had long since pulled from the drive, and the breakfast dishes gleamed freshly washed in the rack. The cloying fog of the dream was gradually lifting.

For a while, drinking her first cup of coffee, she had not been sure if she was asleep or awake. There were moments in the dream she yearned to go back to, but the woman who lived those moments seemed somehow alien. She could not imagine feeling embarrassed in a bathing suit or pretending to be some actress in a movie.

Meredith shook her head, chasing the cobwebs out. Now that she was becoming alert, she felt better. The dream was only one more sign of the loneliness. The beach, the lodge, even the detailed vision of the lobby could have come from a magazine picture. At least she no longer feared him so much. In a sense, by spending beautiful time with the man, she had made friends with the loneliness. In fact, more than friends, if what she remembered from the dream was true.

She sat shocked. Horror lay behind this, and here she was thinking fondly of the man who seemed to be the source of her terror. If this was not true madness, it was surely an excellent substitute. She pushed away the shock and examined her feelings. They were still sexual. She felt a slight tightening in her belly, then laughed at herself. Dreams about sex were normal, and sex seemed to have been the aim of that particular dream.

Meredith rinsed her cup, dried it, and tossed the dish towel down the cellar stairs. It would go into the laundry. She had plenty of cleaning to do if the house was to look good for Halburton's visit tomorrow night. She began listing the chores in her mind: laundry, kitchen floor, polish the silver. The list broke off.

In the dream the man had seemed different, and not just because he felt a little less threatening. It was something about his appearance.

She struggled to recall his face as it had appeared over her, set off against the blue sky. His skin was tan, yet that seemed explained by the setting. He had looked slightly younger, and healthier, too, whatever that meant. Then she remembered. The scar. The man's forehead, when he leaned over her, had looked smooth and unmarred. The scar was not on it.

She wondered what it could mean. Perhaps it was a symbol, revealing her relationship to the dreams. After all, now that she understood them, the man could be a friend, not an enemy. Perhaps the absence of the scar meant that whatever part of herself he represented, it could not longer do harm. That was possible, or perhaps it was something more complex. She would ask Gus about it if she got the chance.

As for now, it was time to get moving on the day's work. Meredith stooped to gather up the pile of used rags that had collected under the sink. They would go into the first load of laundry, and that had better get started.

Her mind focused on the day's work, but as she moved to straighten up, a twinge of uneasiness gripped her. She stopped in midcrouch, her fingers tightening on the edge of the sink. There was something wrong.

It felt reminiscent of the dreams, but it was not a dream. The man was near, and yet she was not dreaming. She was not alone in the room. A flood of awareness hit her, and she felt sexual desire mixed with dread. She had felt exactly this way on Monday during her few hours alone in the house. The man had been present then, and he was near her now.

Meredith pulled herself erect slowly, every muscle straining. She gripped the edge of the sink, refusing to turn, willing herself to disbelieve. She could not. If she turned, she would not see him. She knew that. Yet the man felt as near as he had been in the dreams. He was also as far. She leaned against the sink, trying to grasp how she knew.

There were a lot of things this knowledge was not. It was not a sound or a touch. She did not smell the faint, fruitlike fragrance that had filled the air on Friday. The knowledge did not come from logic, or from the senses, or from anything she could explain. Yet it was real.

The knowledge had clarity, the way a decision felt when it was right. It came from somewhere inside, a place no persuasion or doubt could touch. It was like knowing, like the instant when she first saw Richard on those library steps, that something special could happen between them. It was an intuition, the unexplainable knowledge that someone was watching her, as if a stranger happened to be reading over her shoulder.

Meredith wanted to fight the feeling. Instinctively she knew she could not win. It felt as clear as the everyday certainty that gravity would continue to hold, that the sun would come up every morning.

If I speak, she thought, *he will answer*. She was not

ready for that. Meredith willed herself to turn, to examine the familiar kitchen. When she did, she found nothing more than she had expected.

A pool of sunlight spread over the cloth on the table. The bouquet she had brought home stood in the table's center. The flowers gleamed, reflected in the clean white enamel on the side of the stove. The floor showed dull spots where it needed to be cleaned. She brought her gaze full circle, back to the counter on the right of the sink. From what she could see, she was alone.

The presence remained. It did not diminish, but hovered in the air, eddying, expectant. *What does it wait for?* she wondered. *What can it want?*

A shiver of fear struck her. Suppose the man pressed closer, forcing her to acknowledge that he was there? Instantly she knew he would not. Whatever shimmered unseen in the air, it felt patient. He would wait for her to come to him. And yet there was a certainty in that waiting, a knowledge. She had no choice, and he knew that. She would eventually come.

Meredith looked down. Her hand was shaking. At the moment it did not look like the hand of anyone who was sane. It still held the bundle of rags, their raveled edges squeezing out between the white grip of her fingers. She had meant to take these downstairs and start a load of laundry. Then that was what she would do.

Willing each step, she walked to the door of the cellar and opened it. She flicked on the light and made her way down the stairs, her heels clacking reassuringly against the wooden stairs. The gray concrete cave of the cellar was empty of the awareness, as she had hoped it would be. She took a deep breath and commanded herself to continue. Perhaps if she ignored the uncanny feeling, it would pass. She lifted a pile of laundry and began sorting. Then, just as she began to feel safe, the awareness returned.

The light overhead seemed to grow dimmer. The presence gathered, making the air feel soft, erasing the chill of concrete walls. The presence did not press in on her, as she had thought it might in the kitchen. Rather, it floated sensually at the edge of her thoughts, a whisper like the sound of snow coating a window.

Meredith continued to untangle the clothes, tossing towels and blouses into the two piles. She concentrated on the task as if holding to it, not letting go, would make the feeling pass. It did not. It watched. It waited.

Controlling herself, she measured detergent into a cup and poured it over the clothes. She pulled down the lid, then twisted the dial to set the machine whirring on its first load. She made every movement carefully, as if under the watchful eye of an audience. She stood a moment, hands pressed to the cool metal top of the trembling machine. She tried to figure out what she could do.

She might speak to it. And if she did, he would surely reply. She remembered the reality of Friday afternoon's vision and knew she was not ready for that. No, she could not handle that yet.

She considered leaving. On Monday, the moment she had stepped from the house, the illusion dissolved. Yet the man was doing her no harm. If he suddenly disappeared, if he dissolved as inexplicably as he had arrived, she might even miss him.

Meredith turned and surveyed the empty cellar. She studied the furnace, the shelves lined with Richard's tools, the staircase. The man was only part of her mind, after all. If she could accept that he was her own creation, then maybe she could come to understand what she had created. The fear might pass.

She stepped back from the whirring machine and lifted the pile of white clothes into a basket for the next load. She would go about her chores, trusting the security of her daily routine. If the illusion stayed, she could live with that. To run away, or try to fight it, would only disrupt her life.

The illusion dogged her steps through the remaining hours of the morning. It waited as she passed from room to room picking up things that needed putting away. Whenever she paused for a moment, folding dish towels into a drawer by the sink or selecting silver from the felt-lined box in the dining room, the presence gathered.

Each time it began as a faint hint, a stirring like the first breeze before a change of weather. If she ignored the feeling, it remained formless, a mood, a murmur, eddying close until she moved to the next room. If she focused on it, the illusion grew. It gained shape and solidity, though always lingering on the far side of the tangible. It was never more certain than a cloud or a tune played barely out of hearing.

Throughout the morning, her feelings wavered, rising and falling. Bewilderment washed over her, tinged with awe that she could accept this presence. When she relaxed, her mind chattered on as if engaged in mental conversation with the man. He felt near. Suddenly she would catch herself believing that he was actually there. She pulled back and rubbed her hands over her eyes to dispel the ghostly sense of reality. In that instant the presence withdrew. It would wait, he seemed to tell her. He would always be waiting. He would be ready when she came to him. He would be ready.

* * *

It was this sense, more than the wavering moods, that persisted throughout the morning. At noon, sitting in the kitchen to eat a light lunch, Meredith reviewed the intuitions of the last few hours. The man seemed warm and tolerant. It seemed he loved her. Why, then, did she feel this occasional cold rushing of fear? He would welcome whatever terms she proposed.

Meredith debated whether to speak. The morning hours had been a strain. She drained the last swallow of milk from her glass and remembered she had meant to walk the three blocks to the store to buy another carton. Beyond the window, the day was warm and lovely, but she did not want to leave.

Then she remembered that in this neighborhood women did not walk to the grocery. She remembered that there had been rapes, at least one in daylight; a young girl going to school. She had not thought about them because so much time was spent concentrating on this stranger. She shivered, imagining the shame and fear that schoolgirl must have felt. Then she experienced a real and practical terror that had nothing to do with imagination. She was trapped in this house. The only way she could safely leave was by automobile. She could neither walk away, nor run. There was darkness in this neighborhood, and it was real, not ghostly.

There was a box of powdered milk in the closet. She would mix a quart of that for dinner. She would not go to the store.

Meredith picked up her glass and rose from the table. "Time to polish the silver," she said. The words hung unanswered in the air. She was surprised to realize she had spoken them aloud.

His presence seemed to advance, pressing closer. He

was there and as real, for her purposes, as the sunlight beyond the window. He was as real as a solid weight of the glass in her hand.

"Yes," she said aloud, but softly. She picked up her plate and carried it along with her glass to the sink. "Time to polish the silver."

Her back was turned, but she knew he was watching. When he spoke she steeled herself not to turn.

"Mind if I watch?" It was the same voice that had spoken in her dream, gentle and lighthearted.

"Not at all." She paused, fighting the impulse to scream. To doubt him now would only make him withdraw. She must display courage, must understand what it seemed her mind had created. "In fact, I think I'd like that."

"Good."

The word echoed in the air, or in her thoughts, she could not be certain. It did not matter because she did not want to know.

Meredith tucked the plug into the drain. She turned on the faucet to begin filling the sink with warm water. She felt strangely and fearfully glad. The gladness came from a tiny corner of her mind that seemed to belong to someone else, but fear rode the logical part of a mind that belonged only to her. She and the man would be together, and alone, in the house all afternoon.

Chapter 10

"*Remember that* first day on the beach at Mantazilla?" he asked, a lilt of teasing in his voice. "You burned so bad because you never sunbathed in a bathing suit before. And remember you wouldn't let me rub tanning lotion on your back, because everybody would see?"

Meredith smiled and tried to call up the memory. "I remember faintly," she said. "I remember the last day best, when we went back to our room." She looked through the kitchen window and across the lawn. It was another sunny afternoon, but shadows of clouds crossed the lawn. She remembered the shadows of children at play. Elsa Johnson's house squatted like a troll on the sunny landscape.

It was Thursday. The man had remained with her all of Wednesday. They chatted their way through her chores. Her sense of the man's presence would expand and flourish when they talked of the happy memories she culled from her dreams: the lodge at Lake Mantazilla, the movie theater where they had first met. Only once, when she mentioned the cocktail party that they had left early, did the air seem to darken. Her awareness of the man had faded and a terrible dreariness hedged in to surround her. She quickly changed the subject. Warmer thoughts drove the chill from the air.

"You do remember the first day," the man insisted. "You said we could go back to the room, put on the lotion, then go out on the beach again. But we never got back to the beach, did we?" The man chuckled.

Meredith stood working at the sink, peeling potatoes for the evening's dinner. Gus Halburton would be joining them, and her preparations were well on schedule. By the time Richard arrived home, around six, Swedish meatballs would be simmering on a back burner, their light aroma filling the clean and orderly house. She glanced at the clock and surprised herself as she felt a pang of regret. Yesterday evening, as the hour approached for Richard to come home, her certainty of the man's presence had faded. He had completely disappeared by the time Richard's key turned in the lock, and only this morning, when Richard left for work, had he returned.

When she was with him, the closer to him she drew, Meredith understood that she was changing. Her usual bright confidence, the certainty of success that had carried her through college and her courtship with Richard, vanished like a fleeing ghost. With this man, with this illusion or dream of a man, she could not find a confident bone in her body. Instead, her mind swam in a sea of uncertainties, blurry with vague longings and sudden cold currents of fear, rocked and lulled by forces welling up from some deep sea canyon where she tumbled, utterly unsure of herself or even the direction of her fall.

The man encouraged her in every way, of course. He truly loved her. It was she who shied away from speaking out, from taking risks or sharing laughter.

She'd put on the brown dress to please him yesterday afternoon, and worn it again today even though it was growing soiled. When she buttoned the long row of tiny buttons the dress seemed a shield against a world she did not understand. In this darker, less vibrant color she knew how to behave, how a not very attractive, plain young woman would act around her husband. Meredith found herself stifling her own thoughts—or, actually, this other woman's thoughts—and letting them fall unrecoverably to the sea's floor. And when she spoke, her voice sounded faint. He often asked her to repeat words she had swallowed in timidity.

They had spent the day trading memories. Some of them came back easily, like the lodge and the beach. Others hung back, specters on the edge of her awareness that were unwilling to come to the surface.

"Yes, I do remember," she said suddenly, a scene from memory filling her mind. "But we went back out on the beach. That night, after dark. And you wanted . . ." She caught herself and the words trailed off. The scene was too embarrassing to recall.

"That's it, 'moonburn.'" The kitchen chair creaked as he leaned back in it, laughing. "I wanted us both to suffer third-degree moonburn. On every inch of our bodies."

He had said the words to embarrass her, and Meredith felt a blush rise to her cheeks. Blushing was one of the odd things about being with him. She never blushed or felt shy in Richard's company. She loved Richard, and loved making love with him. There was nothing to be shy about. But now, with this stranger, she had not felt so self-conscious since high school.

Nevertheless, it felt pleasurable to have the stranger near her and adoring her. The man enjoyed tossing out flirtatious comments, although he kept his distance, seated at the kitchen table. There were moments when she could almost see him from the corner of her eye. If she closed both eyes and focused on thoughts of him, he would appear, stretched comfortably in the chair, toying with an apple he had taken from the bowl of fruit on the table. Once she had felt so sure of his presence that she turned to make a remark. The bowl of fruit was not there. Nor was he.

"I never wanted to leave that place, Mantazilla." She pronounced the name wistfully, letting its bubble of sound rise into the light. "It was so elegant. No, so grand, that's the word. I didn't think I belonged there."

She paused, meaning to go on. In these moments, when she felt shy and uncertain, a young girl's thoughts echoed faintly in her mind. If she caught the words and repeated them aloud, the man seemed to understand.

His deep voice interrupted her thoughts. "That's what I love about you. Why, even when we were buying this house, you got all embarrassed. I only called the room upstairs the baby's room."

Meredith felt a wave of shame surge upward. Why did she feel embarrassed? A flood of memories carried the feeling. She recalled that she and the man were standing in the upstairs hallway, and the real estate man was there. She was uncomfortable as her husband joked with the real estate man about having babies. Her grandmother had always said ladies did not discuss such things in front of men.

"My grandmother," she said, dazed. "I just remembered something."

"Her." The voice behind Meredith spit the word in disgust. "She belonged in a museum. All those stories, girls getting pregnant from kissing a boy. And then sending you to that girl's school."

The man sounded angry and he did not stop. He complained harshly about a woman Meredith felt sure she had never met. The grandmother sounded like a relic of Victorian days, an ancient crone who terrified children with old wives' tales.

Meredith listened in awe. She recalled both of her grandmothers clearly and they were nothing like this. She remembered the sweet nostalgia of Christmas at their homes when she was a child. But the woman he described was nothing like them.

"I hardly remember her," she said at last when the man paused. The memories seemed as if they were not hers at all, but those of another woman. And when that woman stirred inside of her, she felt overwhelmed and pushed down, drowning in her own smallness and insignificance. She thought of parents. Surely the other woman, that shadow hazing over each of her thoughts, had parents.

"My mother and father," she said timidly. "What about them?"

"What a crime." She heard a sigh at her back. "You were so young when they died, and that witch took over."

Meredith reflected on what she had learned. This was far more real than the dreams. She wanted to be tough minded, to quiz this man and find out everything he knew. She felt as if a young simpleton were living inside her. This girl had other memories, other experiences, an entire undersea life utterly different from hers.

Nevertheless, she felt afraid. If she turned on him, if she began asking questions and tried to find out too much, he might fade from her thought. She did not want to be without him ever again.

Perhaps if she let the awareness of this other woman well up in her, the memories would return. She would know all about the parents, the grandmother, and the man himself. He would seem real at last, a genuine lover she could see and touch.

"Yes, I was too young," she said tentatively. She waited for the young girl's words to take shape in her mind. "I'm glad I'm here now, though. I'm glad I'm with you."

She waited. The words hung floating in the air. He was supposed to respond but did not. Meredith tried to envision him sitting behind her as he had been only a moment ago. She recalled his gray-green eyes, the sunlight glinting off the red highlights in his hair.

"I love you," she said, speaking aloud again. The words reverberated through her, and they were true. She heard her own voice, but she felt some other woman's feelings churn inside her flesh. That woman did love him in every part of her being. Still he did not respond. Instead, darkness and cold momentarily washed over her. Even beyond the windows the day seemed to go dark.

Perhaps she had said the wrong thing. She could no longer feel his nearness. Something had driven him away. Suddenly she heard a harsh rapping. She spun and saw that Elsa Johnson's red knuckles were rattling the glass window of the back door. The older woman's pie-round face pressed against the pane, staring.

Quickly drying her hands, Meredith hurried to the door, stunned by the interruption and the man's sudden absence.

"Well, I should say," Elsa bustled into the kitchen. "I knocked for a good half minute. Are you losing your hearing?"

"No, I-I must have been dreaming," Meredith stammered. "Sorry."

"And talking to yourself, too? I saw your lips move. Oh dear, perhaps I've come at the wrong time. Well, look at you, in a new dress, too. Please go right on, don't let me interrupt."

In open contradiction to her words, Elsa settled into a chair at the kitchen table. She pulled off her red woolen cap and tucked it into a coat pocket. Then she slipped the coat from her shoulders and let it fall over the chair.

"After all, if you have company, I can go."

Meredith's heart fell. Mrs. Johnson had positioned herself for a view of the hallway that led to the living room. She clearly thought someone had been standing in the doorway.

"Oh, no," Meredith said as lightly as she could. "I do talk to myself sometimes. I suppose I was singing."

"I see." Elsa cast a poorly concealed glance toward the hall. "I was only on my way to the store and thought you might want something. Of course you can tell me to leave if you have a visitor."

"Elsa!" Meredith turned away in exasperation. "If you want to walk through the house, go ahead." She picked up the last potato from beside the sink and peeled away a shred of skin before dropping it into the pot.

"I only wanted to help," the older woman said petulantly. "I came to see if you wanted anything from the store."

"I appreciate your stopping by. It's just that I'm expecting company for dinner. I have everything I need. But thanks."

"I suppose you have a lot to do?" Elsa asked tentatively. "You could walk along. To the store, I mean if you wanted to see where *it* happened."

"Beg pardon?"

"You know. The incident. What I heard on the radio. I think I know exactly where it happened."

"You're talking about a rape," Meredith said. "It isn't the first rape around here." Then a thought occurred to her. "Elsa, are you afraid to walk to the store?"

"I can take care of myself. Only trashy people have to worry about things like that."

"I'm sorry, but that isn't true," Meredith murmured. "There is something awful going on in this neighborhood. In fact, there's a man who stalks around here at night. I saw him." She realized that she had made a mistake. Now Elsa would gossip about her, and how she went out at night.

"I see," Elsa said with grim satisfaction. "But I am not trash, and I don't need to worry."

"Then I really do have plenty to do," Meredith said. "I hope you'll excuse me."

"By all means, go on." Elsa slid her cap from her coat pocket and shrugged into her coat. "Men!" she said with a sigh. "You never can trust them."

Meredith wanted to let the remark pass, but as she held the door for Elsa she could not help reacting. "I'm not sure what you mean. I certainly can trust Richard."

Elsa turned, her coat pulled tight around the folds of her waist. "Oh no, dear. I was thinking of someone else. I'll tell you about it sometime. And of course I was thinking of what happened at Economy Grocery." She turned away with a bright smile and stepped cheerfully around the side of the house.

Meredith stood for a moment, perplexed, but thankful

that Elsa was gone. Then she pulled the door shut against the cool air that was settling in with late afternoon. She leaned against the door, struggling to regain her disrupted train of thought.

Whatever was that woman's goal? Meredith wondered. Or was Elsa simply full of whisperings and hinted gossip to keep people guessing? She supposed that was it. Anyway, thanks to Elsa's poor timing, the stranger had vanished. Meredith no longer felt like the young, untried girl whose words she had spoken only moments ago. The whole thing was getting too bizarre. It might be time to talk about it with Richard.

She checked the clock and realized she should go upstairs and change clothes before Richard got home. She remembered Gus. Perhaps now that she felt more at ease with the stranger, Gus Halburton would not find her thoughts so easy to read.

Meredith crossed the kitchen, flicking on the overhead light against the gathering dusk. From the shelf in the hallway, she grabbed a pair of Richard's jeans and two towels that needed to go upstairs. She stepped into the living room and reached to turn on a light to dispel the gray hovering darkness. Then she stopped. She stood stunned, unable to scream.

The walls were gray. In the dim light, she could see furniture, but it was not hers. A short black couch sat at right angles to the far wall. It faced a pale gray chair in the exact position from which she had moved it last weekend. Between the two pieces stood the dark bulk of a coffee table she had never seen. A row of books lined the mantel, replacing the two silver candlesticks she had polished only this morning. The room was entirely changed, filled with the wrong things, and with an entirely wrong feeling. A spirit floated here, terrible in its agony.

She felt a memory. Grief, like an echo, issued from vast gray emptiness. It was a dark well of cold air, a chasm of grief, and it had something to do with Elsa. It also had something to do with the stranger. The grief was like a vast gulf, trying to absorb her consciousness, and it was fierce with the violence of love. It sobbed with pain, trembled with anger.

Meredith stumbled back against the side of the stairway. The ridged edge of the step cut into her spine. There was death here. No other word could describe the icy fingers that wrapped themselves about her mind. Paralyzed, she felt it gather. The coldness of death seemed a layer across the gray walls, and within the walls—as if she were seeing something happen underwater—the form of a woman stood screaming.

Meredith grabbed the edge of the staircase. She clutched it with her fingers, remembering that it must come to an end. At the lower edge of the stairs was an opening, and she had to get to it. Meredith fumbled along the banister while her mind fought to repel the vision.

It crackled in the air, a dark electricity. It was huge, powerful, and it grasped after her and tried to pull her into that gulf of grief. She reached the step, then spun, reeling into the wall.

The front door stood on the other side of the dark living room, too many steps away and too heavy to open. She pushed away from the wall and stumbled toward the dining room, as though swimming through air that felt far too heavy. The patio doors on the far wall would provide an escape, if only she could reach them. Her hip collided with a sharp edge, and she heard china clatter against silver. She remembered with surreal relief that she had set the table earlier, but it seemed unbelievable that it could still be there. Yet the patio doors were solid and real as she threw her weight against them.

Her fingers struggled with the cold lock, twisted it twice the wrong way, then yanked it back. The door gave. She felt a comforting rush of air as she pushed out onto the patio and slammed the door at her back.

Her breath came in short, desperate gulps. Groping unsteadily toward a chair, she grabbed its cold aluminum arm and sank down. The vision of a screaming woman whirled about in her mind. The face of the stranger, of Elsa, of people she had never known, all surrounded that image. She tried to make some sense of the maelstrom, but nothing fit together. She only knew that she had seen death, that death had been present in that room. The whole thing made no sense. It would make sense if she were crazy, but she understood, feeling the cold aluminum arms of the chair, that the true horror came because she feared that she was sane. She had been like a child playing a pretend game. But this was no game.

Chapter 11

Two hours later, seated in the dining room, Meredith watched Gus Halburton, who sat at the far end of the table. His solid bulk and strong presence almost made her deny the truth of what she knew. Halburton was a scientist and he was her teacher. He stood for rationality and lucid explanations. Even the physical size of the man seemed almost too large for the confines of their small dining room. He took a bite of bread, his gaze intent on Richard, who was explaining the hierarchy of Mabton's electronics industry.

Meredith watched the two men, relieved that they talked so easily. The chill of sitting outside for forty-five minutes was beginning to fade from her limbs, but she did not feel like holding up her end of the conversation. She had been relieved when talk turned to Richard's work.

The panicked vision that had sent her stumbling through the dining room and out onto the patio haunted her thoughts. She had stayed on the patio for a long time, huddled in a cold aluminum armchair. The blue sky faded to an orange haze as the sun went down, then slipped into the purple blanket of gathering darkness.

She tried to sort out her thoughts, but the images would not come clear.

Whatever had happened, it had to do with Elsa Johnson's visit. It also had to do with the man in her dreams. Every time she tried to bring the two images together, they would not join. Elsa knew nothing of the stranger, nor did she ever appear in the dreams. Meredith told herself that the older woman had jarred her from a fantasy and caused the vision of anger and despair. The explanation felt shallow. It could not account for the horror that had kept her shuddering with fear and cold on the patio until the headlights of Richard's car turned into the drive.

She had let herself in the house then, her heart pounding, and hurried upstairs. From the second floor, she called a greeting to Richard and managed to remain there until only a few moments before Gus arrived. When she crept down the stairs again, meeting Richard for a hug, she stared over his shoulder. The living room looked as normal and warmly lit as she had prayed it would. It was filled with familiar furniture, and on the mantel the two silver candle holders gleamed where they belonged.

"So then you've got some freedom, troubleshooting for the company." Gus Halburton's deep voice called her back to the present. "They send you between the departments and you make the decisions."

"That's part of it." Richard's face glowed with enthusiasm. He leaned forward in his chair, describing how he consulted with department managers and helped coordinate their projects.

Meredith felt a pang of envy. It was easy for him, stepping into a ready-made community in this new place. If Gus was right, she herself needed exactly that: work to do and people to be with during the day. If she had those, this fantasy with good dreams and nightmare days might go away. The imaginary man would wither and disappear. Meredith dropped her napkin on her plate to cover the uneaten portion of her meal. She hoped the men would not notice that she had hardly touched her food.

"And what about you, Meredith?"

Meredith looked up to find Richard and Gus both looking at her.

"Given any more thought to starting up a practice?" Halburton studied her, perplexed by her silence. "Don't tell me all this shop talk about electronics has swayed you from counseling."

Meredith forced a laugh. "Not yet," she said. "Actually, it's interesting. Richard's work is a lot like mine. Troubleshooting."

"Mine, too." Gus leaned back and pulled a pipe from his coat pocket. Meredith rose quickly to clear the plates and bring an ashtray. She searched her mind for a topic to keep Gus talking.

"Speaking of work, did you get that reading done?" she asked. "You promised to tell us all about parapsychology."

"Well, now that." A sparkle came into Halburton's eyes as he puffed his pipe, then cradled its bowl in his large palms. "In fact, Meredith, I'm beginning to think my judgment was too hasty."

Meredith stepped to the sideboard, listening while Gus explained the nature of last week's conference to Richard. She sliced three wedges from the cherry pie she had baked that morning and laid them on the delicately patterned bone china plates. When she had set desserts in front of Richard and Gus, she carried her own to her place at the table.

"And the reading?" she asked as she sat down.

Gus finished describing how experts, gathered from throughout the world, had spent three days delivering papers on research into unexplained mental phenomena. Richard's interest, betrayed by his avid gaze toward Halburton, seemed more than merely polite.

"The reading. That's what got to me." Gus took a bite of pie and chewed thoughtfully. "At the conference I heard all about results. Results can be a lot like ghosts, if you'll forgive the pun. Then can come out of thin air. To trust them, you've got to go back and find what's really in the evidence."

"And?" Richard had nearly finished his pie and shot a glance of appreciation toward his wife. "Did you find any ghosts? The real thing, I mean."

"One," Halburton said firmly. "I found plenty of other things, too—sloppy laboratory practices, border-line research, a few interesting possibilities, but only one genuine and reliable study of trustworthy phenomena. Fellow from England did it. I can't argue a single point."

At the conference, he explained, he met a young scientist who worked in brain-wave research. The man had received a grant to study families that had recently lost a member to an accident or disease. He had interviewed nearly a thousand people. Then he monitored the electrical patterns of their thinking, both in the laboratory and at their homes.

"The difference can't be explained by being at home. He tested families that were not bereaved. No similar pattern showed up. Then you figure in the age of the one who died, and the circumstances. There's a rare twist in the alpha pattern. From the interviews, this British fellow could practically predict it."

Gus described how the irregular pattern appeared with

amazing frequency in the relatives of those who died young and unexpectedly. It confirmed research that other speakers had done, and what psychics had been insisting on for years. Those who died young or in emotional turmoil could apparently have unusual effects on the minds of others.

"Clever research, too," Gus admitted. "He double-checked by bringing complete strangers to the families' homes. No relation, no knowledge of the deceased. The same alpha sequence showed up every time. Sometimes stronger, sometimes weaker, but always there. Every time."

Gus stopped speaking and scanned the faces of his listeners. Meredith looked away. The speculation struck too close to home, and she fought to suppress the chill that made the hair on her scalp prickle.

"Come now, Gus." She struggled to make her tone mocking. "Surely you're not falling for ghost stories and hauntings and things that go bump in the night. You of all people."

"Meredith, that is not what I said." The rebuke commanded her to meet his eyes. They were stern, fixed on her with uncompromising authority. She was sure that he suspected something was wrong. She had told him about dreams, but had not told him about the manifestation of a strange man.

"There is evidence," Gus said. "In some cases. Notably those of premature, unexpected deaths, or when a person was suffering an emotional disorder at the time of death. Looking back now, I see where the explanation may fit." His tone softened, but the authority had not left it.

Meredith desperately wanted to disbelieve him. How could Gus, careful, skeptical scientist that he was, accept such things? Of course, he was getting old. An old man, thinking of his own death, would be more inclined to believe in the afterlife. She felt immediately ashamed of the thought.

"But, Gus, you're a scientist," she said at last. "Science accepts new information, but it has to make sense. This doesn't tally with anything we've discovered."

"Not so." Gus picked up his pipe and lit a match. "That was what I was about to explain. It does fit, if you look at the right pieces. We know in psychology that bonds between people can be the most powerful things in the world. Family bonds, bonds of friendship. Even the bond a Good Samaritan accepts when he stops to offer help."

"So what does that have to do with it?"

Richard cut in, annoyed at her interruption. "Gus is trying to explain. Listen a minute, darling."

"Human beings have responsibility to one another." Gus resumed his slow analysis. "We know in schizophrenia that if one person cares, if only one person matters to the patient, there is hope for recovery. I'm not the scientist to say bonds like that cannot survive death, or even exist before birth. You're a counselor, Meredith, you know the first rule."

Meredith nodded absently. She saw where Gus's argument was leading, and did not want to go further.

"The first rule," Richard asked.

Gus waited, watching for Meredith to respond. She stared down at the untouched slice of pie on her plate, reviewing the words. They were the first Halburton had ever spoken to her, the opening of his introductory lecture on interpersonal psychology. Over many hours of helping clients, she had learned that they were true, but they could not mean what Gus asked of them now. Even as she spoke, she could not believe he was right.

"Need never belongs to one alone," she said at last. "If I know about it, it is mine."

Gus waited a moment, then responded to Richard's perplexed stare.

"Simply put, it means we are responsible to do our best for those we find in need. We cannot do everything for them, and we should not. But when another member of our species needs something he cannot get alone, and when we know that, he is no longer alone. We are with him, seeking it together."

"You said, 'another member of our species,'" Richard broke in. "What does the rule have to do with those who are dead, prematurely or otherwise? I don't get it."

"Neither does science. We cannot say precisely when life begins or ends. I do believe each life has purpose. From this research, I must consider the possibility that when that purpose is unfulfilled, the spirit, the quickening of nature that makes a life, may linger. I can't say why it is, or how. But I can admit the possibility."

He had been responding to Richard, but Meredith knew he was watching her. Now he turned. "Can you, Meredith?"

"I can't argue with what you've said. I would like to see the evidence. You've got to admit, Gus, it's pretty farfetched."

"Agreed, but if the evidence held up, and let's assume that it does, could you accept it?"

Halburton's gaze grew uncomfortably penetrating. He saw her to a depth she did not want to acknowledge. "As a possibility," she said at last. "A possibility, that's all."

"Of course."

The words formed a frost on her heart. They made her think of the stranger, of Elsa, of the coldness of death she had witnessed that afternoon. This could not be, she told herself. Yet she had just admitted that it could.

Chapter 12

Lately Meredith had been dropping off to sleep with ease, and tonight was no exception. After the conversation with Gus, the afternoon's vision, and more than anything, the day in the company of the stranger, her strength felt sapped. The moment her head touched the pillow, sleep surged up. She fought it for a moment, drawing back in fear from the dark edge of unconsciousness that was encroaching. The man waited there and she did not want to go to him, but the dream was strong. It pulled her downward, as if her limbs had no strength; a slow but enormous wave that dragged her under and into his arms.

The dream began at Mantazilla. She knew they were there, although she did not recognize the room. The walls were patterned with blue-and-white paper, and sunlight spread a diffuse haze through the curtained windows, making everything sparkle.

The air was warm. Her skin tingled with a radiant glow, as if she had just emerged from a pleasantly stinging shower. Each nerve felt separately alive, sensitive to the smooth coolness of the sheet beneath her, to the soft pillow cradling her neck, to the warmth of his hands gliding over her skin.

Meredith looked up. The man's eyes were closed, and his lashes were light, feathered brushstrokes above his high cheekbones. In the hazy light, the flush that had come to his cheeks glowed like faint flames against his pale skin. His lips were pressed to a thin line, and the intensity of his expression drew his skin taut, making the delicate bones of his jaw stand out.

The man leaned above her, supporting his weight on his arms. A froth of blond hair sparkled on his chest, muscles rippling faintly beneath it. The skin of his shoulders and arms glistened with a light film of sweat, and his body heat, like a hot wind blowing from the desert, stirred her senses. His movement pressed her ear to his chest. Deep inside, she heard the harsh rhythm of his breathing and the pulsing of his heart.

They were rocking, rocking, like a small boat braving a storm. Meredith's own breath came in sharp gasps, forced from her by the strength of his movements. A warmth began in her thighs and spread rapidly upward over her hips to ignite a hot glowing cone in her belly. It flared and raced out to her limbs, her flesh, her emotions. This was love. He was bringing it to her. She loved him with all the desperation of his blows against her hips.

She gave a sharp cry as he thrust deeply one last time and spasmed against her. She closed her eyes, and the darkness shone with a bright, shimmering glaze. The dream washed over her like a wave, tumbling her senses and tossing her upward to drift aimlessly in deep, velvety warmth.

She did not know how much later it was when the dream resumed. She awakened to the urgency of his lips. His body moved in slow and sensual rhythm against her breasts and thighs. She looked up and fell into the ocean of his gaze.

Chapter 13

Meredith awoke exhausted on Friday morning, her body a deadweight that had to be dragged from bed. Early in their marriage, she and Richard would sometimes make love all night. She could remember fatigue, but not exhaustion such as this.

Downstairs, she managed the habitual movements of making Richard breakfast, then saw him off, excusing her sleepy silence as exhaustion from preparing for Halburton's visit. Richard kissed her lightly on the cheek, but his look showed concern. He urged her to go back to bed.

It was raining outside. She wished she could give in to Richard's suggestion and to the narcotic effect of the rain tapping on the roof. She could not. The yard sale was advertised for tomorrow, and nothing had been prepared. Even more, all through the night she had been making love with the strange man to whom sleep had somehow betrothed her. She remembered his gestures, the glistening of light on his skin, and her own helplessness against the passion he aroused in her. She could not sleep, would not sleep, she told herself. Sleep meant falling back into his arms, which even now seemed to reach out for her.

The house was muggy and warm, so she pulled the back door open, latching the hook on the screen. Fresh air and hard work would wake her, and if they did not, she would perk a pot of coffee as thick as tar. She turned to the task of pricing the miscellaneous grab bag of items set aside for the sale.

The shelves of the pantry were full. Clothes from college and Richard's little league coaching equipment filled one large box on the floor. Elsewhere lay three sets of barbecue tools, wedding gifts that had never been used, the scotch plaid cooler, and tablecloths that did not fit the new table. On another shelf were old clocks, extension cords, an outdated encyclopedia, two cookbooks, and the odds and ends of cloth from an overambitious quilt project. Meredith pulled a roll of white sticker labels from her pocket and debated how to set prices.

The point of the sale was to meet the neighbors, and people might be offended if she set prices too high. Bargains seemed best, so friendship could trade on goodwill. Meredith wrote seventy-five cents on a label and pressed it to the side of a picture frame. She dusted the glass before turning to the next item.

The work went quickly. Within an hour she had priced and dusted many of the smaller things, arranged the encyclopedia volumes alphabetically, and sorted through a stack of records to be sure there were none worth keeping. While she worked, she had time to think. It was a pleasure to work alone, feeling strong and self-sufficient without giving in to imagining the man's company. Gradually, relief dawned on her. The stranger's presence did not seem alive in the house this morning. In a sense, like the echo of another woman's emotions, she missed him, but that would probably pass. It might be that the whole business of loneliness would now pass. Maybe those dreams of making love were the culmination. Maybe life would return to normal now.

On the other hand, maybe it would not. She reviewed the evidence. She remembered back to the first dream, how each had brought the man closer and closer. Then came the talk with Gus, and after that at least her fear diminished. Nevertheless, in the days since, the man had not faded from her mind. If anything, he became more real, keeping her company as she moved through the house. The awful vision that had occurred in the living room yesterday seemed linked to the growing reality of his presence.

The really frightening thing was how she seemed to change when he was around. She knew herself, and she was a confident and competent person. But when he was around, she felt herself slipping away, melting into someone much younger and more self-conscious. Even in last night's dream, she had seemed unable to express her full adult sexuality, her pleasure wrapped in her own fragile helplessness, overwhelmed by his power and experience at lovemaking. She had been like a small cloud driven to and fro by bursts of wind.

Meredith paused, a tablecloth half-folded and forgotten in her hands. Color rose to her cheeks. Even now her thighs ached at the memory of his touch. The rain had grown heavier, and it beat a hypnotic rhythm outside the back door. Its drumming insistence made her long for sleep and for the sensuality of the dream. She took a deep breath and let it out slowly. She would not give in, not now. She could at least hang on to the world of daylight. Perhaps if she spent one day alone, in full control of her life, his power might fade.

Meredith finished folding the cloth and stuck a tag on it asking a dollar-fifty. The scotch plaid cooler and

stepladder would both be bargains at three-fifty apiece.
At least if she did not make money, she intended to make
friends.

The rhythm of the rain was steady and peaceful. Its
tapping on the lids of the trash cans outside the back door
accompanied her work like an irregular sort of music;
sometimes soft and predictable, sometimes loud and
persistent. She had grown so used to it that when she first
thought she heard someone calling she dismissed the
sound as rain. Wind rattled the screen door, reminding
her of Elsa's visit. She felt glad, because at least bad
weather had a way of keeping busybodies at home.

The sound came again. It definitely sounded like a
man calling.

"Hello. Hello there. Can you hear me?"

Startled, Meredith looked up from the bookend she
had been dusting. She was about to turn when she heard
the voice call more audibly.

"Are you there? Please, can you hear me?"

Meredith stiffened. It was the stranger's voice. She
tried to deny it, but there was no mistaking that deep,
gentle tone. She was stunned. There was nothing other-
worldly about the voice. This could not be illusion.

She tested the air for his presence, but he had not felt
near all morning. Even as she whirled and surveyed the
pantry, she sensed no hint of his company. Yet, he had
spoken.

"Please don't," she said, in a low whisper. "Please,
please, go away."

A knocking rattled the screen door. The voice called
again. "Mrs. Morgan, I'm Arthur Watson. I called. Mrs.
Morgan?"

The message suddenly reached her. This was the man
who had called the other night about the yard sale. She

had told him to come Friday morning. Without setting down the wooden bookend, she hurried into the kitchen to see a tall man in a raincoat and wide-brimmed hat barely visible beyond the rain-soaked screen. She rushed to open the door.

"I'm sorry," she exclaimed in embarrassment. "I didn't know it was you. I mean, you must have thought you had the wrong house."

"No, I knew the house." Arthur Watson dipped his head to remove his rain hat and then pressed his handkerchief to his damp face. He looked up and said, "But I wasn't sure you were home." He seemed hesitant, almost as if he wished he were not there.

At the first glimpse of his face, Meredith stumbled backward against the edge of the sink. The bookend dropped with a sharp crack and she heard splinters ricochet from the baseboard. She stared at the man from the dreams.

Chapter 14

The man's hair was dusky brown and his eyes shone an intense gray-green. His high cheekbones and the fine line of his jaw glistened with dampness. As he looked at her, the small crescent-shaped scar above one eyebrow reddened perceptibly. The man was somehow embarrassed, maybe even afraid, but she could not see why that should be.

The day seemed normal. Somewhere a car honked, and in the distance a small airplane droned. The silent neighborhood seemed poised and waiting, but then the neighborhood always seemed that way.

"Mrs. Morgan? Are you all right?"

Meredith gasped. Was she all right? Words lost their meaning with this man standing across from her. What was she going to say? *I spent all night making love to you?* She had feared this man, then had made love to him. He had caressed and moved against her body.

"Here, let me get that."

He stooped and began gathering the broken remains of the bookend. With his head turned away, Meredith tried to tell herself she was only imagining the resemblance, as she had imagined his voice calling a moment ago. Yet the same voice spoke now, stammering an apology for having startled her. The similarity was too strong. Either the illusion had finally appeared in the flesh, or the man in her dreams actually straightened to his feet in front of her now.

Meredith knew she should speak. She tried to find words, but fear and fascination overcame her and she merely stared.

"Perhaps I should go," he said hesitantly, looking as if he wanted to run away. He laid the splintered wood on the counter.

"Oh, no. Please. I'm sorry," she stammered. "It's just that I, I'm sorry, you look like . . ."

"Someone you know? People say that a lot. Common face, I guess. I didn't mean to scare you."

Meredith moved to retrieve the chips of wood, then drew back, holding them, frightened by the power of his nearness. "No, I'm sorry. Are you sure we haven't met? I mean, *have* we met?"

The man's brow furrowed. "Maybe around Mabton. Live here all your life? We, that is, I did."

"Actually we just moved here. From up north a month ago."

"Then it can't be." The man's lips widened in a smile. "I've been out of town all month. Job interviews. I explained why I wanted to sell"—he paused, then hurried on—"to sell a few things? I mean about going to Europe for my job?"

"Oh, yes." Meredith let the shattered remains of the bookend drop into a trash bag. She felt as if she were playing a part in a bizarre play, suddenly thrust onstage, uncertain of her lines, but compelled to act a scene she could not quite remember.

Her heart fluttered and her skin was damp with a light sweat. She felt embarrassed that her hair was messily tied back by a scarf, that her work clothes were smudged and gritty from the dust in the pantry. She glanced around the kitchen. Everything was reassuringly normal, red flowers arranged on the table and the breakfast dishes drying in the rack. It was all the same, yet entirely different.

"You brought things to sell," she said stupidly. "I guess you want to bring them in."

The man noticed her glance at the room. "The kitchen looks wonderful," he said suddenly. "I like the color."

"Of course, you could bring them in here." She realized the import of his words. "Oh, you mean the new color. Have you been here before?"

He looked quickly away. "No, of course not," he fumbled. "I figured, I mean, since you just moved, looks like new paint."

Meredith studied him. The man was lying, and he wasn't a good liar. She could not figure out why he was lying. He avoided her gaze.

"Well," he said, squaring his shoulders, "better get moving. Did you want the boxes in here?"

Meredith took a deep breath and tried to gather her thoughts. The intimacy of last night's dream welled up in her, a powerful undercurrent beneath the roles they seemed to be playing. Never before had she felt attracted to another man, but the awareness of his body felt like the approach of an enormous wave, beautiful but deadly. She imagined him returning with the things he had brought, then settling down in the kitchen for a cup of coffee.

"No, on the patio. I'll open the doors," she blurted out. "You go ahead. I'll be there in a minute."

"Some yard sale you'll have if this weather keeps up. They say it'll clear later, though." He pulled on his hat, pushed open the screen door, and was gone.

Meredith's legs felt weak as threads. She leaned heavily against the side of the sink and stared at the reflection her face cast on the rain-spattered window. She looked terrible. Her lips were pale and all the color had drained from her face. Wisps of dark hair trailed from beneath the edge of her scarf, and a smudge of dust shadowed one cheek. She hesitated to look down at the shapeless, faded overalls she had chosen to suit the morning's work.

On an impulse, she hurried to the bathroom. She kept a small makeup kit there and as she hastily scrubbed her face and applied a dab of lipstick, she wondered faintly why it mattered. The man outside was a total stranger, perhaps only resembling the one in her dreams. She felt guilty, but could not resist the impulse to free her hair from the scarf and comb it quickly into place. As she stepped onto the patio moments later, she no longer felt afraid that the man would find her plain and unattractive.

He was handsome. She had paused to study him through the glass door before turning the knob, and the illusion, if it was an illusion, persisted. Arthur Watson was the man in her dreams, slightly older perhaps, but the same. He looked tired, as if worry or travel had prematurely aged his features, and his clothes were a bit too large. She wondered if he had recently lost weight, but his movements were strong and agile as he lifted a heavy carton onto the patio table. Meredith felt a pang of regret that she had not invited him to bring the boxes indoors.

"There you are," he said. "I hope this is all right. I mean, piled out here. And that it's not too much. You're doing me a favor, after all, I don't want to impose." His words trailed off, embarrassed at the flurry of apology.

"No, that's fine. I'm glad you brought them."

They stood facing each other, Meredith fascinated simply to stare at him, his gaze mild but perplexed. The moment lengthened into awkwardness, carrying the odd illusion of two statues posed within a rustling curtain of rain. Meredith's heart pounded. She wanted to reach to him, pull his body hard against her own and hold on tightly. The need felt urgent and obvious, as if doing anything else would be dishonest. She willed herself to remain still, to behave normally and say something. No words came. Her thoughts felt muddy and vague, eerily uncertain like the thoughts of a young and timid girl.

"I'll get the last box." He turned suddenly and stepped back through the transparent curtain of rain. He walked to a small yellow car parked in the drive.

Meredith glanced at the cardboard carton that lay open on the seat of a lawn chair. On top were two wooden napkin rings, a few pearl gray linen napkins, and a copy of a popular paperback on child rearing. The book looked well thumbed, but as she surveyed the other boxes she found no children's toys or small clothing. One carton held only kitchen items: wooden spoons, a spatula, two plates, cups, and glasses. She wondered what had happened to make him sell off his household. Divorce? Of course he had said he was moving to

Europe. Perhaps it was cheaper to start anew than to pay for air freight.

Footsteps splashed on the walk and Meredith drew her hand back, pretending to be busy arranging space for the last box.

"There, that's all of it." He slid the last carton onto the table. "This one's mostly books."

Meredith tried to remember appropriate words. "You put prices on?"

"Thought I'd better not. I mean if you don't mind, just take what you think they're worth. Or whatever people offer. I know this is an imposition . . . if you'd prefer, I could stay out here and write some." Arthur Watson seemed as confused as she was. He sounded apologetic.

It was her turn to speak. The man looked at her, but words seemed like distant memories she could not quite recall. She remembered the dream. This was exactly how she had felt fumbling for something to say in his company. She was the young girl at Mantazilla, embarrassed even to speak, sure that whatever she said would be wrong. She could feel her own knowledge fading behind the wooziness the other mind cast over her own.

I am Meredith Morgan, she reminded herself. *I am a capable professional counselor. I am not some timid little girl.* "No, that's fine," she said. "I'm pricing anyway. Can you come by Saturday?"

His intense eyes widened. "Saturday? No, I can't, I'm busy. Why?" He seemed nearly frightened.

"But you want the proceeds?"

"Oh, yes, the money. That's right. Listen, you take half. More, if you don't think that's fair. You can mail me a check." With relief, he pulled a small vinyl booklet from an inside coat pocket. He tore a sheet from the back and extended the slip of paper to her. "I'm leaving Wednesday, but it should get there in time. If you don't mind mailing it Sunday . . ."

"I'd be glad to." Meredith's fingers shook as she withdrew the deposit slip and stared at the address. The hand she had taken it from belonged in last night's dreams, gently caressing the tips of her breasts.

Meredith took a deep breath and concentrated on what she should say. "I'm really happy I could help. Lucky you saw the sign out front just when you had things to sell. Assuming, anyway, that I sell anything."

The laugh she forced came out too high, but Arthur Watson seemed not to notice. His gaze traveled past her to study the cartons on the table.

"Mind if I sit down?" Without waiting for a reply, he folded into a chair. His hands gripped his kneecaps as if bracing against a wave of emotion. "It was lucky," he said quietly. All the strength seemed to have drained from his body.

"I hope this is the right thing," he said at last, looking away from the cartons. "Sorry, my wife and I, we're, uh, no longer together. I guess this is harder than I expected." His face failed to conceal a sadness that was alive and immediate. His mouth hardened with control, but he was near tears.

"Of course." Meredith heard her best professional tone enter her voice. She remembered many of the clients she had helped through painful divorces. "Can I get you a glass of water? A cup of coffee? You should come inside, Mr. Watson. I'm being rude."

"Arthur, please. No, you've been kind enough." He

pushed himself firmly to his feet. "I have to pick up airline tickets, pack, run all around town." He gave a small, tired laugh. "Anything that doesn't sell, I mean you could, uh, anything that doesn't go, maybe Goodwill? Or keep it for yourself." He winced at the words.

"They won't be thrown away," Meredith assured him.

Arthur smiled and pulled on his hat. "Thank you, Mrs. Morgan."

"Meredith."

"Thank you. Meredith." He turned and walked back into the rain.

Meredith watched him get into the car. He waved once through the windshield, and the small yellow car backed from the drive. As it disappeared up the street, Meredith sank into a chair and covered her face with her hands. Her fingers were icy cold.

He was gone. He had been right here, the exact man, and he was gone. Terrible loneliness mixed with grief cut through her. She tired to pretend he was still there but the illusion would not take hold. She was alone. Only a moment ago they had stood not three feet from each other, and now he was gone forever.

She pulled back the flap of the last box his hands had touched. A plaid wool shirt lay beneath a handful of books. One of his shirts. She yanked it loose and pressed the rough wool to her face, breathing in its scent. Tears welled up. Meredith wept into the cloth, which had a faint fruitlike fragrance. She sobbed, and it also seemed that sobbing was coming from the dark gray living room, an inconsolable grief.

Chapter 15

Meredith drove. She let impulse set her route, meandering through the peaceful streets of neighborhoods, turning off when the boulevards became crowded with stoplights and shops, taking a ramp to follow the highway for a few miles, then looping back to enter avenues crowded with apartments and corner groceries. She watched the gas gauge drop and paused on a street near Mabton State to fill the tank. She thought of stopping to see Gus, but got back in the car and kept driving.

The aimless wandering did not make her peaceful, but it was better than staying at home. It was better than struggling for words to make Gus understand. No words could express the bone-chilling loneliness that fell over her when Arthur Watson's car drove away. No words could explain why she could not bring herself to enter her own living room.

She had fought against it for a while. She hardened her will and managed to tag a few more items in the pantry. She fixed a light lunch but found she could not eat, then thought of going upstairs to make the bed. She rejected the thought because she would have to pass through the living room and because the rumpled sheets carried reminders of last night's dream. Loneliness followed her, with a sigh at the close of every gesture, like a cold black cloth draping each object she touched. She had grabbed her purse and jacket, then hurried to the car.

Rain blurred the windshield and left tear traces along the path of the wipers. One wiper caught at each stroke, letting out a small, weeping cry. The loneliness sat beside her, a silent passenger who refused to meet her eye but inwardly blamed her for letting him go.

Meredith tried to ignore it, playing the radio loud, then shutting it off in a rage at the disc jockey's stupid chatter. She focused on driving, but the turns and stops came automatically, leaving too much of her mind free to want him. Now she concentrated on memorizing the scenery, reading the name in front of each store, thinking of what might be sold inside.

Brenner's Delicatessen had signs advertising sour-dough rolls, baklava, and pickled herring. The sign on Sunny Day Cleaners promised In and Out—Only Four Hours. Top Stop Tavern sold beer, wine, and sand-wiches. The street looked familiar, as if she had been there before, and she recalled the stoplight at the corner. Meredith eased on the brake as the light changed.

The sidewalks were lined with stone steps leading up to apartment buildings. She remembered the name of a film playing in a neighborhood she had passed, and glanced up to see it advertised on a marquee half a block ahead. The sign on the corner said Dimont Street. Dimont. Surely she had come past this intersection of Thirty-second and Dimont three or four times already. The light changed and she pressed down on the acceler-ator.

She was driving in circles. How had she gotten here? The neighborhood was to the east of Mabton State, but she had never been here before today. Suddenly she remembered. One hand guided the wheel as the other fumbled beneath her jacket.

The slip of paper rustled loose in her overall's pocket. Small printing at the bottom of the deposit slip said 3225 Dimont, and she leaned forward to stare through the windshield before pulling to the curb in the middle of the block. Number 3225 was painted in white on the side of a red brick building across the street.

Meredith leaned her forehead against the rim of the steering wheel. So this was where the drive was leading to, as if she had been deliberately searching for him. The realization felt strange, but no more strange than the dreams. Now that she had found Arthur Watson, given that all the reasons for finding him were mad, sitting in an idling car across the street from his apartment felt sane. It made crazy sense.

Meredith looked through the windshield at the neighborhood. Soot-blackened brick buildings and small shops suggested the area was poor, but it hardly looked dangerous. The flower bed outside 3225 was well kept, and in the windows of the three-story structure a few flower boxes stood in front of clean white curtains. Meredith watched an old woman ease a shopping cart down the front steps. The woman reached the sidewalk and, pulling the cart behind her, headed toward Brenner's Delicatessan. Perhaps Arthur Watson would soon walk through that door. Meredith wondered how she would react.

If he did not appear, she could invent a question about the things he had brought, and then go inside and look for him. She shuddered at the thought of being alone in his presence again, this time not even in her own home. What would she say? Could she hold back the impulse that insisted she reach out to him, pull him into her arms and press his body close?

She could not go. She had only come to see him again, to make sure Arthur Watson was actually the man. Her excuse felt weak, but it allowed her to stay and she accepted it. The loneliness was real and present in the car, throbbing like the idling engine, a steady beat beneath each of her thoughts. Meredith turned the key and the engine died. Somehow being on streets that he walked each day, among people who possibly knew him, she felt as if they were together. The windshield wipers gave a final, weeping complaint as the engine died, then came to a rest while fat drops of rain filled their paths. Meredith leaned back in the seat and looked out the side window. Sooner or later Arthur Watson had to appear on the steps across the street.

After two and a half hours, the view from the front windshield had faded behind a fog of condensation. Using a tissue that had been made damp from many wipings, Meredith swabbed a porthole clear on the side window. She could see the side mirror, part of the street, the steps, and the doorway of the red brick building.

Few people passed. The old woman had returned an hour ago, limping, her shopping cart a heavy load to be lugged up the steps. Cars passed, but none of them were the yellow compact Meredith remembered seeing in the driveway that morning. The clock on the dash said 4:10. Arthur Watson had neither come in nor gone out.

Meredith reached for the key to start the engine, but the gesture broke off in futility as it had each time she tried to leave. If she went home, she would find only the emptiness she had come here to escape. Besides, if she waited until Richard came home, perhaps the house would feel safe once more. She set the damp tissue down and glanced at the side mirror. The street seemed sodden with neglect or sadness, not with rain.

The street reflected the delicatessen window and the blinking red sign above the doorway to the Top Stop Tavern. The sign flashed like a warning or like a beacon to souls who endured evenings by drinking through the afternoons. A figure was coming through that door, and as she watched, he turned to shake hands with another man. The two men waved to each other, and then one broke away and began walking in her direction. Meredith recognized the black raincoat and wide-brimmed hat. Arthur Watson, his shoulders hunched against the rain, approached on the far side of Dimont.

Meredith's hand closed automatically on the door handle. She yanked it down, but suddenly the figure in the side mirror stumbled and lurched toward the side of a building. He caught his balance on a stair railing and walked on unsteadily.

Before she knew what she was doing, Meredith heard the engine roar to life. She slammed the car into gear and felt a jerk as the tires squealed from the curb. The windshield was a blur, and she swabbed at it madly. She accelerated past an amber light, which went red as it disappeared at the top of the windshield. Buildings and signs raced past, shimmering reds and yellows that rippled in the rain.

He was drunk. The man was drunk and he would hurt her. Hands would rip her clothes, and the stench of alcohol would press against her mouth as surely as a man's body would force itself into her. That wasn't possible, because this was the man in her dreams. At the same time the drunkenness sent its own terrifying message. She had to get away before his face, terrifying and ghoulish as some grotesque rubber mask, came up to the side window. She had to escape before his hand closed on the door of the car. The vision of him reaching out for her, tearing at her clothes, taking her against her will, flooded her mind.

A horn sounded beside her, but she did not hear. She saw a red light, signaled, and swung into a right turn. She had to escape. In the instant before the car had started, she felt a clear premonition of a man—Watson maybe, or any man—yanking the car door open and pushing his way inside. Her wrists had been pulled from the wheel and a weight forced her down. She could not see his face—his face was distorted and horrible—but his mouth closed over hers, smelling of alcohol. His tongue pressed her lips open and she tasted sweet sickliness.

Meredith saw two red lights flashing at a railway crossing. She pressed the brake and hurtled forward as the car bucked and lurched to a stop. The engine died. In the sudden silence she heard the deep-throated groan of a train whistle and the rattling of cars. An instant later, a silver engine roared past, followed by a bleary rainbow of passing cars.

She must go home, she realized. She must do that or drive to Mabton Electronics or call Richard; find him somehow. She could no longer live alone with this madness. She would wait for him at home, and when he arrived, no matter what it cost, she would tell him what had been happening. If she could find the courage to explain, he would understand.

The last car of the train rumbled past. The guardrail lifted as the bell stopped clanging, and Meredith pressed her foot to the accelerator.

Her legs were trembling, her whole body shaking with

fear. She took a deep breath and scanned the street signs for the highway turnoff that would take her home.

That evening, after the dinner dishes were washed and put away, Meredith returned to the unfinished work in the pantry and admitted that some decisions were easier imagined than carried out. She had seen it happen a hundred times with her clients, men and women who left her office week after week resolved to change jobs, discipline children, or ask for the divorce that had been postponed for years. Week after week they returned, mute and discouraged, unable to muster strength to make the decision a reality.

Tonight she knew how they felt. Her reasons were a lot like theirs, and no doubt equally tissue thin. Tonight did not seem the right time, a Friday when Richard's tired face and distracted silence showed his exhaustion after a week's work. The truth should probably wait until he returned from the trip out of town. Perhaps it would be wrong to tell him at all—especially now, when they were thinking of having a baby. She could think of nothing more cruel than suggesting love with a complete stranger.

Except that when Richard was near, she did not feel that way at all. Sometimes it seemed that two women lived inside her mind. The first woman, Meredith, was deeply in love with her husband. The second woman, a timid girl, was charged with every kind of emotion there was when it came to Arthur Watson.

The list of reasons to postpone speaking was as long as her arm, and probably just as weak, she thought, lifting a box of old clothes from the pantry shelf. She could wait for the perfect moment forever, and it might not appear. Yet one reason felt stronger than all the others, and now, thankful that she had a moment alone, Meredith examined that one.

Until a moment ago, when the doorbell rang, Richard had been helping her in the pantry. They were not expecting anyone. Richard had gone to answer the doorbell, assuming it must be the paperboy. Now Meredith listened to the sound of voices from the front room and debated whether her best excuse was merely an excuse, or if it made sense.

Her best excuse for keeping silent about Arthur Watson was that things had seemed different when she returned home. The loneliness was gone. She had pulled into the drive only a minute before Richard. The twin beams of his car's headlights caught her as she turned her key in the lock. She waited, entering the house beside him. The darkened rooms were chilly and damp, but no more dreary than a rainy evening might make them. She glanced through the patio doors and saw Arthur Watson's cartons still there, then walked through the house, turning on lights and straightening the half-made bed upstairs. The blankets and sheets no longer suggested her long night at Mantazilla. In fact, in the pleasant lamplight, the dream itself seemed rather silly. The empty rooms of the house felt perfectly sane, tidy from Thursday's cleaning and reassuringly calm.

Now she listened as the voices in the living room broke off and the front door closed. She remembered how her lover's presence had always faded before Richard came home. When Richard was with her, she never felt like that shy young girl; frightened and without will. Now she and Richard had two days together, a weekend of safety that might allow her time to figure things out. Relief washed over her. Meredith pressed a price tag to a sweater and folded it into a box. All the other excuses were lame, but not this one. Arthur Watson's appearance, and even the terror of seeing him drunk, seemed like recollections from another world. She would say nothing about it unless the right moment arrived, because for now at least she had peace of mind.

"Guess who that was?" Richard's lanky frame filled the doorway to the pantry. He held a thick sheaf of papers.

"How many guesses do I get?" Meredith smiled and pushed the carton of clothes to the back of the shelf.

"It was Gus Halburton. He says hello, but he didn't have time to stop. You can guess what he came by to drop off."

Meredith's heart sank. She should have known Gus would not leave last night's discussion unfinished. "Papers from the conference," she said flatly. "That British report."

"Bull's-eye." Richard loosened a rain-spattered plastic sheet from the papers and separated printed sheets and pamphlets. "He needs it back Monday. I promised we'd read it over the weekend. He says you aren't required to analyze the statistics, since you hate them so much. Would you look at these numbers?" Richard held up a legal-size sheet thickly stripped with columns of numbers. "They're all explained. He said to check out the case histories."

"I haven't got time right now." Meredith gestured toward the array of half-finished projects spread over the pantry. The mess was deceptive, since most of the work was done, but she would gladly do it over again rather than read about ghosts.

"Gus seemed to think you'd find them interesting," Richard said. "He seems worried, and I think he's worried about you. He wondered aloud if I really need to make the trip." Richard's concern was so obvious that it made her fear for both of them. One word from her and he would cancel the trip.

She could not have that. Seven years of happy marriage came at least partly because she was as independent as Richard. He was the kind of man who would sacrifice a job, a house, or anything else for her. He did not realize how much she already depended on him. She had to keep the balance right between them.

"Gus and I are working something out," she said honestly. "It has to do with the move to a new town, with work, and us having a baby. I'll get it sorted out."

"You're sure?"

"I've never lied to you." She hesitated. Maybe concealing things was a way of lying. "There's some relevant information, supposedly, in that material Gus gave us. I don't think I need it, but he thinks I do."

"You work," Richard said, "I'll read. That way we both get to hear." Meredith wanted to protest, but stopped. Richard skimmed the titles of the pamphlets. "Case histories," he announced. "Seventy-one Interview Summaries Correlated with Alpha-Wave Divergence. Don't worry, I'll just skip the dirty parts." Richard joked to cover his concern for her.

Meredith smiled. "Three. I'll listen to three. But nothing too scary—it's close to bedtime."

Richard's fingers flipped pages until he reached the middle of the bound yellow volume. "Case forty-three. No, that looks dull. Try forty-four. 'Alpha-wave divergence persistent and significant, see appendix,'" he began reading. "'Decedent, a fourteen-year-old female, pregnant out of wedlock, infection resulting from non-sterile abortion.'"

"Richard, that's grisly."

"I'll skip that part. Here we go: 'Family members complained of hearing movements in the daughter's room at night. Investigated to discover toys moved and a previously open window closed. The room was cold. Mother experienced repeated dreams in which the girl asked to talk to her father. Father concealed grief beneath anger at the daughter's pregnancy. They had argued the day of the daughter's death. The girl would not reveal who had gotten her pregnant. In dreams, the daughter told mother that the father should not seek identity of the man, and he definitely should not seek revenge.' "

Meredith wanted Richard to stop, but she also respected Gus. She knew that she must hear this. The case history was impassive enough, without half the violence she saw regularly on television. "Could you read one without a dead child in it?" she asked. "That makes me sad."

"Me, too." Richard skipped ahead, glancing rapidly through the pages. He stopped two-thirds into the book. "This looks easier to take, death from natural causes. 'Deceased was an eighty-three-year-old male who died in his sleep.' Sound bearable?"

Meredith nodded. She scribbled a price on a carton of records instead of pricing them separately. If the work got done quickly, perhaps they could go up to bed.

"Okay: 'Family living in the house at the time of death consisted of son, daughter-in-law, and three grandchildren. Alpha divergence weak and unstable in adults, growing stronger as ages of children decreased. Youngest child, age seven, believed that the grandfather was angry at the father about a red tractor. He claimed grandfather came into his room every night and told him this. The father owned no farm equipment, but recollected after questioning that thirty years before, when he was an adolescent, he had ruined his father's tractor. Of special interest is the mental condition of the grandfather at time of death, diagnosed two years earlier as dementia praecox.' " Richard sounded the words out and glanced at his wife. "Brain disease?"

"Schizophrenia. It's an old word."

"Schizophrenia, two years before, huh?" Richard read on. " 'Deceased had become obsessed with the idea that his son should be punished for numerous imagined evils. Deceased apparently tried to persuade the child to hate his father.' "

Richard looked up and shook his head slowly. "Spooky. I mean, about punishing, and then the kid knowing about the tractor. Of course, there could be an explanation, old scrapbooks, grandpa telling the kid. Still it's spooky."

Meredith slipped past him, carrying her dust cloth to the sink. The case histories gave her chills, but Gus was right about their fascination. She wanted to believe and disbelieve them at the same time.

Richard skimmed ahead. "You said three. Read one more?"

Meredith nodded mute assent.

"I'll skip the gruesome details," Richard said. He explained that the case was a suicide by a woman twenty-three years old. " 'Subject lived with her parents and had been depressed by home situation, caring for both parents' chronic alcoholism. Numerous absences from work had caused her to lose her job. The mother ceased drinking at the time of the death, and had continued sobriety to the time of the interview, one year later. She said the daughter became confused on the day of death, insisting there was no difference between love and hate, life and death. Daughter complained she did not know which was which anymore.' "

"Sad," Meredith put in. "So young and so hopeless."

"Apparently she wanted her parents to stop drinking," Richard went on. " 'Mother's alpha pattern showed no divergence. Father's pattern diverged on one occasion, when he was interviewed and later tested out as blood alcohol level point one-oh. He said the daughter would not leave him alone, kept whispering curses to him whenever he drank. Subject appeared disoriented, belligerent, confused . . .' Whoa, here's a kicker." Richard scanned the rest of the case study. "When the man finally dried out, the daughter began whispering about guilt. The father eventually was a suicide, too."

Meredith sank into a chair at the kitchen table. The case histories sounded cold and impersonal, yet she could easily imagine how the subjects had felt. Her own visions and nightmares suggested what it was like to feel truly haunted.

"I'm sorry, I just got interested." Richard closed the volume and laid it on top of the others, then stepped closer to knead the muscles above her shoulders. "Are you okay?"

"It's all right." This was the moment, Meredith realized, if there was ever going to be a right moment. The descriptions of hauntings made her own experiences seem almost plausible. Perhaps Richard would understand.

Meredith fought to make her voice calm and to choose the right words. "This stuff bothers me more than it ought to. I've, well, been having a bit of emotional upset myself. Gus helps."

Richard's hands moved from her shoulders to massage

the nape of her neck. She felt the skin pull tight against a hard knot of tension.

"You should have told me. I got involved with the new job and wasn't paying attention."

Meredith leaned her head back and looked up. His eyes were warm and concerned, filled with the love she knew she would find there. A troubled look darkened them. Richard was feeling guilty, taking blame on himself.

"It's what we talked about, isn't it? I mean having a baby. I've been pushing too hard, and then to hear stories of teenagers dying of abortions, old men haunting children. Damn, I'm sorry."

Meredith opened her lips to speak, but he hurried on.

"Darling, you should go back to work if you want to. If you're not ready, I'm not. I pushed, and I apologize."

Meredith's head fell forward. She gave in to the gentle pressure of his fingers, and her resolve failed. Richard lived in a world filled with real things, with having or not having children, with doing jobs, earning money and spending it. His world did not include obsessions, terrifying dreams, or visions that came out of nowhere.

And it should not. Richard had a right to the predictability of his world. She loved him, but love did not give her the right to turn his world upside down. The secret made her lonely, but she was glad she had said nothing.

"Let's go to bed," she said, covering his hands with her own. "I feel like cuddling up next to you."

Chapter 16

Saturday morning dawned fresh and dazzling blue. Meredith awakened early, alert after a deep, dreamless sleep. She had not felt so good in days. On the other hand, she had not been without dreams for the preceding several nights. She did not know what had made last night different, but she was grateful. She hurried downstairs to fix an extra-large breakfast. Night seemed to have chased the storm from the sky, and with it, as impermanent as the weather, went yesterday's cloud of fear. By the time Richard wandered into the kitchen, Meredith felt buoyant. Arthur Watson's things would be sold today, and once the check went out in the mail, she would probably never think of him again. Nonetheless, Richard still seemed concerned about her, and about their talk of the night before.

"It's a beautiful day," she told him. "If there was a problem I think it's gone."

They lingered over breakfast, enjoying the luxury of time together, but at last they rose to the task of carrying cartons and card tables out to the yard. The grass was still spongy from last night's storm, so they lined the front walk with tables and spread plastic tarps beneath the larger items on the lawn. By ten, everything was arranged, a colorful array of goods spread over tables and planks on sawhorses. They settled down to enjoy the remarkable morning and wait for customers.

Earlier, they had confessed to each other their worry that no one would come, but before long that fear turned out to be groundless. Elsa Johnson appeared first. Meredith watched Elsa's blue colonial down the street. She was not surprised when, within a matter of minutes, a curtain in the side window moved and the door swung open. Elsa called to someone in the house, then slammed the door and hurried up the street.

"That man is so slow," she said, reaching the central table. "I told him to be ready at ten, but he has to read every word of the paper."

Meredith and Richard exchanged amused glances. They had agreed that Elsa would be first, and she would probably handle every item. A twenty-five-cent bet rode on what Mrs. Johnson would buy; Richard said one item, Meredith predicted no sale at all.

They had not figured on the questions Elsa would ask. As new customers began to appear, emerging from houses along the street or alighting from cars, Richard took responsibility for Elsa. He moved with her along the rows of tables and planks, explaining that the encyclopedia had been a graduation gift from his parents, that the quilt scraps were all there, pinned and matched, but needed to be sewn.

Meredith remained at the central table. She counted change and fielded questions and introductions. As she expected, the other neighbors knew one another and they greeted her warmly. The people across the street, whom she had glimpsed only briefly going to and from their cars, turned out to be Claire and Jonathan Miller. Both worked, and both were friendly. Meredith accepted an invitation to dinner for the following weekend.

From farther up the street came a quiet couple, the Cupplestones. Janet Cupplestone fell in love with an antique radio Richard had once bought but never had time to fix. She warmed to Meredith and, while Andy Cupplestone's back was turned, asked to have the radio set aside. She would pick it up later and have it repaired for her husband's Christmas gift.

"Can I get it Thursday? I've got the morning off." Janet worked as a bookkeeper in downtown Mabton.

Meredith slid the purchase behind her chair. "I hope you'll have time for coffee."

Janet accepted and exchanged a conspiratorial wink with Meredith as her husband approached.

The sale was going well. The first rush of bargain hunters had combed through the boxes, stopped to visit at the sales table, and carried off treasures. Now the crowd began to thin, and Meredith leaned back, thankful for a moment to catch her breath. She watched Richard straighten items on the tables and fend off Elsa Johnson's questions. So far, Meredith reflected, she was winning the bet.

Elsa had inspected over half the merchandise and bought nothing, insisting that her husband would be there soon with the money. At last the door of the blue colonial opened again, and Elsa's hand lifted to cup her mouth for a loud, "Yoo-hoo, over here." She returned to the task of sorting through old books and remarking on the Morgans' taste in reading.

Mr. Johnson was solid looking. Meredith told herself that anyone married to Elsa had better be solid. He was large and muscular, but starting to go to fat like an aging football player. His shoulders were heavy, his face thick.

"Ed Johnson," he said, extending his hand toward Meredith. His eyes left her face to travel quickly over her figure. He was mentally undressing her and was not even trying to hide the fact. For a moment his presence made even the beautiful morning turn ugly. He gave a low whistle of approval. "Hope my wife hasn't bought out the store. I'm not in the market for anything except a few girlie magazines."

Meredith smiled uncomfortably and eased her hand from his grip. It was not yet eleven o'clock on a Saturday morning, yet she could swear she smelled a faint odor of whiskey. She decided to put him down quick. "Girlie magazines are for teenagers," she said. "There aren't any teenagers in this house."

"If you're really holding a yard sale," Ed Johnson persisted, "you need girlie magazines and a kissing booth. Like the old county fairs."

He paused, as if checking to see how far he could go. Meredith did not respond.

"Don't mind me," he added without hurry. "The missus keeps me in check. Just trying to make friends with the neighbors."

Meredith looked away at the sound of Richard's voice. He and Elsa had progressed to the far end of the row and now he held up a brown skirt and a plaid hunting jacket.

"Where did these come from?" Richard said. "They don't have prices."

Meredith glanced down at the carton. "Arthur . . . ," she began, then stopped herself. "That man brought them. Remember he called? Take whatever they're worth. He said it doesn't matter."

Meredith watched Elsa's eyes widen in surprise. Elsa glanced from Meredith to Richard, and then toward Ed Johnson.

"Whatever they're worth," Elsa's husband interrupted. "My wife will want them for ten cents."

There goes the bet, Meredith thought. She excused herself and moved away to straighten a table, putting a wide berth between herself and Mr. Johnson. The older man began to browse through a box of paperbacks, and Meredith smiled to herself. He would be a long time searching for torrid titles in that box.

Toward the end of the table, Elsa seemed to have lost interest in the cartons Arthur Watson had brought. Her brow furrowed in concern. She leaned close to Richard, confiding something and nodding once or twice toward the house. Probably more gossip about the former owners, Meredith thought, and was relieved that today was Richard's turn to get an earful.

Casually, so she would not be noticed, Meredith eased back toward the central table and sat down. A few new customers moved along the tables, but she felt most curious about Elsa's husband. There was something familiar about the man. He was certainly unpleasant enough to make a strong first impression, but she couldn't recall meeting him before. Perhaps she had seen him at a neighborhood store, or coming home from work. Up the street, the Johnsons' lawn looked ragged, but perhaps she had seen him mowing it. Yet his raspy voice sounded familiar, too.

Her attention was drawn to the house across the street and a few doors down from the Johnsons', as its front door opened and a tall woman emerged. Above a forest green kaftan, long red hair gleamed in the sunlight. When the woman turned to stride down the walk, Meredith was struck by her poise and self-confidence.

So this was the owner of the sports car that occasionally appeared in the driveway. Meredith had wondered who had enough style to favor such a car in this solidly middle-class neighborhood. She instantly liked the woman.

"Mind if I look around?" a cultured, bell-like voice called out as the woman came into the yard.

"By all means." Meredith debated whether to go over and introduce herself. She glanced toward Richard but saw that he had suddenly turned away from Elsa. He passed rapidly between the rows of tables, his eyes dark and his movements abrupt. He stepped around Mr. Johnson and moved on without a word, kicking an empty carton sideways before dropping into the chair at Meredith's side.

"What's wrong?" she said in a low voice. "Too much of Elsa?"

"I don't know how you put up with the old bat."

His cheeks were pale with anger and his hands were clenched in fists at his sides. Richard shot a glance toward Mr. Johnson's back as the older man moved up the aisle to join his wife. Meredith studied her husband. He seemed too upset for Elsa's cat-and-mouse games.

"Did she get going on the people who used to live here? She pulls that on me. Ignore her, it makes her mad."

"She spared me that. Let it go, okay? I'm about to throw her and her old man off the property. Great way to meet the neighbors."

"She isn't that bad."

"Want to make another bet?" Richard was furious.

At the end of the row of tables, Elsa and Ed Johnson huddled over the box of clothes Arthur Watson had brought. Now that she no longer had Richard's attention, Elsa pawed through the goods in earnest, lifting each item for her husband to see.

"Our nosy neighbor," Richard went on, "must be leaving footprints in people's flower beds."

"What could be that bad?"

"Insulting you, for starters." Richard had been pale with anger, but now color returned to his cheeks. "She insulted you and I resent it. I told her to peddle her trash somewhere else, once I got the point. First it was the little barbs, about you having visitors during the daytime, and didn't she know who, too? She put it so innocently. I thought it was this yard sale buff, what's his name? Watson. So I went for the bait. That's when the lecture started, all about how untrustworthy husbands and wives could be, except her and Edward, of course. She suggested that you had enough affairs to occupy ten women. I told her to go push her shopping cart. Over a cliff."

Meredith remembered Elsa's suspicions of the other day. Before she could speak, Richard turned to her with a grim smile.

"You'll probably get the lowdown on my sex life at work. She manipulated me into describing my secretary and half the file clerks. I only caught on to her when she asked if I found any of them attractive. Can you believe it?"

"I can and do," Meredith said flatly. She nudged Richard to silence. Mr. and Mrs. Johnson had joined forces at the end of the aisle and now, Mr. Johnson carrying the scotch plaid cooler, they moved toward the central table.

"Looks like I lost the bet," she whispered.

Richard hissed his reply. "Prices are going up."

Ed Johnson hung back a few steps, studying Meredith while Elsa approached the table. "I cannot believe you are asking three-fifty for this cooler," she began. "I'll offer two, cash of course. It probably leaks."

"Four-fifty," Richard said firmly. "If you want the lid, too, it's five."

"Five!" Elsa tipped the metal bucket sideways to examine its bottom. Meredith felt embarrassed. The tall red-haired woman was approaching, carrying a handful of books and she had obviously heard every word.

"I can go to five-fifty, if you're really interested." Richard persisted. He was beginning to enjoy himself.

Elsa's husband ignored the exchange. He had noticed the handsome woman's approach, and now a wide grin broke over his features. He started to close an arm around her shoulders.

"Sally Fielding. Well, it's been a dog's age."

"Keep your meat hooks where they belong," the woman said. She moved deftly from beneath Ed Johnson's arm and extended her hand to Meredith, but Meredith hardly heard her. She suddenly remembered where she had seen Ed Johnson before.

The likeness was unbelievable, yet too close to be wrong. This was the man who had greeted Arthur Watson in her dreams. They had all been together at the cocktail party, and Ed Johnson had insisted on telling a filthy joke. Meredith shuddered against the sense of dread momentarily surrounding her. Elsa's husband was the last person she wanted to see in her dreams.

"All right, three-fifty," Elsa's voice interrupted her thoughts. "But I'll throw in the quilt scraps to make up the difference. Call that fair."

Richard opened his mouth to object, but Meredith nudged him beneath the table. Elsa had already turned to retrieve the box of fabric. More than anything, Meredith wanted them both to leave.

"Three-fifty?" Ed Johnson counted the exact change onto the table. He smiled and gave Meredith a wink. "Could have told you the wife would get her money's worth. Married twenty-five years; twenty-four and a half of them because I couldn't afford the alimony."

He turned and followed his wife from the yard. Their two figures looked exactly matched, bumping along with the purchases.

Meredith felt caught between shock and fury. Surely she must have met Ed Johnson before, but why would he appear in the dream? The older man was repulsive, completely the opposite of the stranger, of Arthur. She tried to concentrate on the mystery, but felt Richard's anger seething at her side.

"That was theft," he said in a low voice. "The money makes no difference, but she just picked up something and walked."

"Laugh it off and forget it," Meredith told him.

Sally Fielding's lilting voice broke the tension. "Gets to you, doesn't she? She's good at it." Sally gave an elegant toss of her head toward the Johnsons' house. "Don't let her win, that's the neighborhood motto. No marriage is safe if you let that bitch win anything. Nothing she'd like better than to see you two fight about those quilt pieces. Last time two neighborhood kids argued, she was out front selling tickets."

Meredith smiled in spite of herself. She was relieved to hear Richard's laugh as she extended her hand across the table. "Sorry you had to witness that. I'm Meredith Morgan, and this is my husband Richard."

"Don't apologize. Actually it's good to see Elsa in top form, but watch out for Ed. He is no longer welcome anywhere in the neighborhood. I'm Sally Fielding, yellow house over there. Except I'm hardly around anymore. Kind of miss Elsa's neighborly visits"—she made a wry face—"like a dog misses fleas."

Meredith laughed and took the handful of books Sally had selected. She immediately liked this woman. Despite her grace and sophistication, Sally had a sense of humor that was refreshingly down to earth.

"The yard sale's a success in spite of her," Meredith said, handing back the books. "I was beginning to think Elsa was the only neighbor I'd meet."

The other woman's hazel eyes widened in mock horror. "Lordy, that's right, you've been at her mercy. When you moved in I thought of stopping by with a few pointers, honest I did. But then it felt silly, and I got busy with the job. I do interior design. Our company's free lance, but it keeps me jumping." She paused and glanced toward the Morgans' house. "Which reminds me. Elsa caught me the other day and went on and on about you redoing the house. Made like she had the inside track on everything down to the seam widths of the draperies."

Richard laughed and cast a bemused glance toward the Johnsons. "I'll bet she did." He paused. "Sorry about the outburst. She got to me."

"It may have been the first time," Sally said, "but it won't be the last. Elsa is a pain in the ass, but when Ed drinks enough he gets almost dangerous."

"Richard had an overdose of Elsa this morning," Meredith explained. She hesitated a moment, fearful that a professional might find her and Richard's tastes too ordinary, but the temptation to get to know Sally was too great. "Why don't you come in for coffee? Maybe you can give me a few tips."

"Gladly, but I'll bet it's perfect."

Richard agreed to watch the sale for a while. "But if the Johnsons come back," he warned, "Elsa can sell tickets to the show. And she's the star."

Laughing, the two women walked toward the house.

Chapter 17

Ten minutes later, Meredith sat in the kitchen, waiting for the coffee to perk and listening to the sound of Sally's footsteps. Too nervous to accompany a possible critic, she had remained downstairs while Sally Fielding accepted her urging to tour the house for herself. In the few moments they had been together, Sally's lively chatter set them both at ease and filled Meredith in on her neighbor's background.

Sally Fielding called herself a country girl, but she had come to the city to pursue a career in modeling. Charm and posture schools bored her. She soon realized that her first love was the beautiful fabrics and elegant settings models enjoyed. That interest led naturally to interior design, where she met her husband. Mark Fielding, she explained, was out of town this week on a buying trip.

For her own part, Meredith had told Sally the basics about the move to Mabton and her own counseling career. Now, as she listened to footsteps returning down the stairs, she hoped her first impression had not been wrong. If the yard sale brought her one friend in Sally Fielding, it would be worth all the trouble.

"Who did your color selection?" Sally's voice called from the dining room. "I love the Wedgwood blue."

"Actually, I did. I'm afraid it's nothing too original."

Sally came into the kitchen and joined Meredith at the table. "Basic good taste. Lots of lights, lots of color. Not as flamboyant as I would have done, of course. Mark accuses me of favoring eighteenth-century French high-brothel style. I simply love red. It clashes with my hair, naturally."

Relieved, Meredith poured two cups of coffee. "From what I saw when I moved in, anything would have been an improvement."

"Oh, that." Sally's eyes widened. "I never saw the gray, but Elsa talked it up enough. Too bad about what happened."

Meredith studied the other woman. She obviously knew more about the house, but assumed Meredith had the whole story. The opening was too attractive to pass up. "You mean the way they painted the place?"

Sally stared at her in surprise, so Meredith hurried on. "To tell the truth, Elsa's been dangling some secret in front of me for the last month. Every time I ask what happened, she clams up. Did the former owner go crazy, or what?"

"The wife went crazy. And Elsa didn't tell you? Why, the old witch—but it figures." Sally glanced around the sunlit kitchen. "The Johnsons play games. He screws around some with any slut that will have him, and Elsa actually seems to approve of it. Ed pays for his freedom by telling Elsa every piece of gossip he unearths."

Meredith knew that there were all kinds of perverse behaviors, but she was always a little shocked when she ran into a new example. "Feels like the walls have ears," Sally continued, looking around. "Things started getting real bad about a year ago. Gruesome goings-on for our part of town. But Lordy, you've got to live here. Maybe you'd rather not know."

"I think I'd better." Meredith explained that at least the truth would help her fend off Elsa. "And it feels important," she added, "emotionally, sort of."

"Can't say I blame you, but it's not a pretty story. Elsa knows more than I do, but you'll never worm it out of her. Come to think of it, I hardly remember their names. Anderson or Adam or something. Hers was Patty. She always called herself that little girl's name, never Pat or Patricia. Not that I saw much of them. We met once for introductions when they moved in, once at our place a year or so later."

"Don't take it wrong, but I get the feeling you weren't friendly with them. Any reason?"

"I didn't dislike them. We never really talked. He was some sort of engineer, and Patty . . . well to tell the truth I felt sorry for Patty. She was okay, nice enough, but shy! Unbelievable. And she worshiped the ground her husband walked on. Couldn't hold up her end of the conversation if I as much as said a cuss word. Which I do." Sally cast an appraising glance. "Bother you?"

Meredith rolled her eyes. "Hardly. I mean, hell no."

"So anyway, this mousy little Patty wanted to have babies. Nothing but babies, that was all she could talk about. Asked me all about my two, they're eight and ten now. Asking what was it like being a mother, and did I want more kids. You gotta be kidding, I said, which was when the conversation fell apart."

"This was when they were at your house?"

"When they moved in, the first time I saw them. Mark and I were hardly home those days, setting up the business and running around to make contacts. Nosy Elsa poked her head in and gave reports now and then.

Once the sweet young thing was supposed to be pregnant. False alarm, it turned out—wishful thinking, I figure. Anyhow, maybe six months later something awful happened. Elsa lets on like she knows what, but I don't think so. She came by and said the poor little thing was crying one morning. Elsa acted all important about what it might be. I know Elsa, she was trading on credit that time. Shortly after that, the gray went up. Elsa spread the word, natch, and when I drove by I snuck a look through the window. Lordy, you should have seen it. Oh, but that's right, you did."

Meredith nodded. She was saddened by Sally's meandering tale. Memories of gray walls, charcoal furniture, and dark rugs had told of an emotional depression that fed on darkness. "Did she ever get pregnant? Maybe she had a miscarriage."

"Could be. They never did have a kid. Which reminds me, that looks like an extra room upstairs. I assume you have plans."

Meredith had to laugh. Sally's quick, caring way of setting a person at ease and her spontaneous curiosity were a welcome relief after Elsa. "Don't tell Elsa, but we do. Maybe soon." She explained about the debate between children and work. "To tell the truth, now that I feel at home here, I suspect the work will have to wait."

Sally smiled broadly. "I felt the same way, and you know, I was right. Lordy, I wouldn't give up my two for the chance to redecorate the White House." She paused as if lost in thought. "But where was I? Of course, the gray days."

"Did you see her after that?" Meredith broke in.

"Once. Twice, if you count a shape under a sheet the day the ambulance came. Brrr." Sally shivered, shaking her head. "I never saw her out around the yard or anything. But the second time was when Mark and I were having this neighborhood get-together, maybe two years ago, and damn it felt rude not to invite them. We never figured they'd come, but in the door walks little Patty, him behind her. She was wearing this long gray dress, and did it look awful. But she had her chin out in the air, holding her head stiff like some Hollywood princess. I mean, you could practically hear the strain it took for her to say hello. She looked like death warmed over, poor kid. I tried to act nice, 'wonderful to see you both' and all that. But then, oh hell, I checked out. She looked so pale and scared, like any minute she'd fall apart. I ran like a yellow coward and went to pass hors d'oeuvres."

Sally paused, her attractive features suddenly tight with concern. "Anyway, they left early, him hustling her out the door. They even brought the car, half a block, if you can believe it. Of course, they maybe had another place to go. Wonder if they ever got there . . ."

"And then?" Meredith felt riveted to Sally's account. She tried to cover her eagerness by taking a sip of coffee, but found it had gone cold.

The other woman remained silent for a moment, and when she spoke, all liveliness had faded from her voice. "Suicide," she said bluntly. "The poor kid killed herself. Not right after, a couple months. Seems like it was spring. Elsa found the body, the husband was gone at work. To hear Elsa tell it," she added bitterly, "the poor child was swinging in the breeze out on gallows hill."

Sally's words left off. Meredith waited, part of her mind in rebellion against hearing more, the other part, the stronger one, unable to turn away.

"Elsa will tell you her gory version, no doubt, but the

plain truth is she hung herself. From the upstairs railing of the banister, must have jumped over the rail. She was dead when they got there. Really sad."

"It could have been an accident . . ."

Sally shook her head. "Not a chance. The husband left, moved out the next day. No cops investigating or anything. Besides, he really did love her. I mean he must have, putting up with that, right?"

Meredith nodded, at a loss for words. She remembered the air of death she had felt in the living room, the advance of those terrible gray walls. It was impossible, she thought, or possible only in dreams. Or hallucinations.

Gloom descended over the kitchen. Sally seemed distant, lost in her own thoughts. Meredith felt embarrassed.

"I'm sorry I brought it up. Fine way to get acquainted," she added. "This isn't the cheerful cup of coffee we'd planned on."

Sally tapped with the sugar spoon. "Don't apologize. You need to hear. Sometimes I wonder what happened, you know? It must have been something awful. I mean, we all go through rough times. What made her go so far?"

"I think I know." The words escaped Meredith before she realized their meaning. She wanted to call them back, but they were true. "Not know," she fumbled. "Feel? I feel that's it. Moving in and being around all that gray, would you understand if I said I could feel her pain?"

Sally's hazel eyes studied her sympathetically. "I think so."

"I don't mean ghosts. Or maybe I do." Meredith

shook her head and looked away. "Sorry. Listen, you need more coffee. Let me get that."

"No more for me, I have to go." Sally stood and shook the creases from her kaftan. "But let's get together again soon, okay? And next time we won't talk about this, and not even a word about Elsa. Deal?" She paused, smiling as Meredith nodded in agreement. "Say, how's your schedule this week? Mark's gone until Thursday. Got an evening free?"

Delighted, Meredith welcomed the opening. "Richard's traveling this week, too," she said. "He gets back late Wednesday night. Which is best, Monday or Tuesday?"

"Tuesday. Monday's the fabrics convention. How about my place around eight?"

"Perfect."

Sally was momentarily hesitant, seeming to try to make up her mind. "You'll be at home alone for three nights. I don't want to scare you. I saw a phone in the bedroom."

"Yes."

"Door locked, curtains pulled, maximum security." Sally was displeased with what she was saying, but she obviously felt that she had to say it. "I told you that Ed was not welcome anywhere. I saw him in my backyard late one night. Claimed his hat blew off, and he was looking for it. Trouble is, there hadn't been a stitch of wind all day."

"Peeping Tom?"

"That would be a generous explanation." Sally turned as the kitchen door opened.

Richard leaned into the kitchen. "When do I get a break? Fellow down the street wants to show me a boat he is selling."

"There go the profits." Meredith thanked Sally with a smile, then followed her out into the yard. It was a beautiful day, even though the street was deserted except for a few customers in her yard. When she glanced toward Elsa's house, she caught a movement of a curtain in an upstairs window. She paused.

Usually Elsa did her spying from the kitchen.

Chapter 18

The yard sale had been a genuine success. When they carried the tables and boxes back into the house on Saturday afternoon, Richard marveled at how little remained unsold. A few items of clothing had not gone, along with a half dozen books and several of the things Arthur Watson had contributed, but for the most part, purchases had been carried off in twos and threes, leaving less than a third of the clutter that had been stored so long in the pantry.

"Why would people want all that stuff?" Richard wondered aloud, shaking his head over the stack by the back door.

"I gave good deals." Meredith smiled knowingly. "That way people had an excuse to buy and make friends. Every trash can in the neighborhood probably has a piece from our sale in it tonight."

Richard laughed but he had to admit she was right. In addition to the invitation for bridge the following weekend, he had plans for a trial excursion in one neighbor's sailboat and an opportunity to go hunting with two others.

"I'll haul the rest to a Goodwill bin tomorrow," he promised, "but for tonight, how much did we make?"

Meredith spilled the jumble of bills and loose coins onto the kitchen table and deducted a portion to send to Arthur Watson. "Over fifty dollars."

"Easy come, easy go. I'm taking you to dinner. Eat, drink, and be merry, for tomorrow—day after tomorrow, actually—I dine alone in some hotel room up north."

Meredith gripped him quickly in a hug and hurried upstairs to dress for dinner.

It wasn't until Sunday afternoon, after Richard had packed for his flight the following morning, that they remembered the remains of the yard sale.

"I promised to take that to Goodwill, didn't I?" Richard stared down at the half-collapsed cardboard boxes piled in the kitchen.

"We can both go." Meredith helped him carry the collection out to her car and wedge the boxes into the trunk and backseat. They were about to leave when she paused and glanced back toward the house.

"Could you wait a minute?" she asked. "Warm up the car, there's something I forgot."

The engine started and settled into an idle as she let herself back in the house.

At first she could not find the overalls. She had worn them on Friday, the day Arthur Watson appeared, and as she searched the laundry hamper upstairs a sense of panic seized her. She tumbled the contents of the hamper over twice, sure they were there, before she remembered and rushed back downstairs. The overalls lay at the foot of the cellar stairs, flung there Friday night to be included in Monday's washing.

The deposit slip with Watson's address was crumpled deep in a side pocket, but she drew it out and unfolded it with a sigh of relief. The check would go out today, as she had promised, and that would be the end of her concern with Arthur Watson. She had slept well for two nights, hardly thinking of him during the days. She pulled her checkbook from where it had gotten buried beneath the pile of psychological reports on the kitchen shelf and sat down to write the check.

Her hand would not write clearly. The rush of adrenaline from racing through the house made her jittery. Her fingers shook and her palm was so damp that she ended up voiding two stubs before managing to complete the third. She quickly addressed an envelope and slipped the check inside.

She glanced down at the pile of reports Gus had left. Since Friday night they had remained neatly stacked on the shelf, forgotten alongside the enjoyment of the weekend. Now her happiness faded and a premonition of dread gripped her. Beginning tomorrow, Richard would be gone, leaving her alone in the house. Suppose the emptiness returned? Suppose that haunting presence only waited until Richard was gone, then closed in again, its senses as unerring as an animal's? On an impulse, she threw the plastic cover back over Halburton's papers, laid the check on top, and carried the whole bundle to the car.

"What took so long?" Richard rolled down the window on the passenger's side, his gaze perplexed.

"I had to look for something." Meredith handed the package of papers through the window. "Would you mind if I didn't come? Gus's papers can stay in the car so I don't forget them tomorrow, and that letter needs to be mailed."

Richard's eyebrows lifted. "Anything wrong?"

"I have some things to do," Meredith said quickly.

She tried to think of an excuse, then stepped away from the car to prevent any further questions.

Richard shrugged and rolled up the window. He waved once as the car pulled from the drive. As the car disappeared around the corner, Meredith gripped her arms tightly against the late-fall chill.

She had half an hour. Maybe forty minutes, since he might drive by the post office to mail the letter. She hoped it would be enough time for what she wanted to accomplish. She walked slowly through the downstairs, the pantry, the kitchen, the cheerful Wedgwood blue dining room, and finally into the living room. If the stranger wanted to return, he would come now. He might hover in the air, frighten her with visions of gray walls or death, do whatever he liked. She would be safe because soon Richard would be home. It was better this way than waiting; waiting until tomorrow and not knowing.

She pulled the living room curtains closed against the late-afternoon sun. This was where he had first appeared, seated in the armchair with his back to the windows. She quickly slid the chair to the spot it had stood that rainy afternoon, then took her own place on the couch.

The chair, on that faraway afternoon, had seemed gray. Meredith squinted her eyes, trying to envision him through the slitted lashes, but the image would not appear. The room felt friendly and normal.

"Are you there?" she asked the stillness. "Please, if you want me, come now. I'm here waiting for you."

She felt nothing, or almost nothing. Perhaps there was a slight stir of air, perhaps the freshly painted walls lost some of their gleam. Perhaps even that was her imagination. Sitting in an empty room addressing a chair brought only a twinge of embarrassment. There were no echoes. He did not answer. The chair was only a piece of furniture, and the moment an awkward, failed experiment. She quickly pushed the armchair back to where it belonged and climbed the stairs to the second floor.

In the bedroom the smooth expanse of the white spread on the double bed made her think only of Richard. They had not made love last night, but they had wanted to. Too many glasses of burgundy over dinner had made their movements dull and sleepy, more a yearning for close cuddling than lust. Now late-afternoon shadows gathered, and she flicked on the light by the nightstand to survey the room.

In this bed, in her dreams, she had dissolved into a stranger's arms, lost in love for a man who looked like Arthur Watson. Yet in the calm light today, the dreams held no more power than childhood memories, half-forgotten, clouded by all the life that had intervened. She had met Arthur Watson, and he was a nice enough man, but not the sort who attracted her. He was probably even a little boring, once you knew him. He was a man without confidence. She supposed that psychologically, when Richard was gone at work, she had put together a schoolgirl crush on a man who wasn't strong enough to threaten her real world.

Amused, she recalled being told that a woman her age was approaching her sexual prime. If erotic dreams were any indicator, she supposed the prediction must be true and in, in its own way, intriguing. Impulsively, she lifted the control for the electric blanket and switched it on. Perhaps when Richard returned they would slide between the warm covers and enjoy the pleasures sleep had stolen last night. She stepped back into the hallway.

Only one room remained to explore, and she was

about to turn the knob on that door when she remembered what she had been avoiding. She remembered the story Sally Fielding had told. Meredith stepped back to examine the rail of the banister that ran along the top of the stairs and angled right to face the door of the baby's room.

She smoothed her hand along the wooden rail. It was nicked in places, but strongly braced and sturdy enough to bear a grown woman's weight. She stared over the rail and recalled Sally's words. Below, at a distance of perhaps fifteen feet, sunlight shone on a patch of living room rug. All else was open air, an abyss into which a sad young woman had once leaped, ending her life for reasons she could not have understood.

Or maybe she had a good reason that Sally Fielding did not know about. Meredith shuddered. Suppose the woman jumped, hoping the rope would not hold? Suppose she had felt sorry in the instant her body fell through free air? Perhaps it was that death that had cried out its memory last week in the living room. Yet it was not here today. Meredith felt sad for the young wife, but the overwhelming sorrow she had once felt in this place now seemed no more powerful than the fleeting sympathy she felt for strangers in newspaper stories.

There were many kinds of fears, and now Meredith allowed herself to ask about one of them. Could she continue to live in a house where a woman had killed herself? Forget about ghosts and hauntings. Forget about torrid dreams, she told herself. Could she handle the shadows that must always play around the history of this house?

She thought she could. She was, after all, a trained professional who understood logic and events. If she had been troubled here it was because she was confronting a mystery within herself. The house was not to blame for anything, it was only a house.

On top of that, she admonished herself, people couldn't go selling and buying houses every time wind creaked in a shutter. Richard had a good job, but selling and buying cost money. Richard did not have time—nor did she—to be uprooted now. She decided, as she had decided when she first heard the story, that she would say nothing to Richard about the suicide.

Meredith turned and pushed open the door of the baby's room. It was this room she and Richard had debated longest over, deciding how to decorate, what color of paint, and whether to leave any furniture and make it a small den. Studying it now, she felt glad they had left it empty. The hardwood floor shone russet beneath a coat of wax, and clean white walls waited for the day when it would be right to put up pictures for a child. A low maple chest sat in one corner, its drawers empty but lined with yellow paper. One day small clothing and toys would fill those drawers. One day soon, Meredith thought, if she wanted it that way.

She remembered Sally Fielding's words about children. Sally was a lively, active professional woman but she had insisted on having kids. A wave of tenderness washed over Meredith for the child who was waiting, not yet even conceived. Only she could bring it into the world. She remembered the calendar in the kitchen and mentally counted backward through the days. Richard wanted a child, and if her monthly cycle held true she would be fertile now.

Fertile. She turned the word over in her mind, savoring its suggestions of ripeness and growth. It sounded as beautiful and rich in possibility as a line of poetry. Quickly she closed the door to the baby's room and hurried downstairs to double-check the calendar.

Ten minutes later, when she heard the sound of the car in the drive, Meredith felt calm and certain of her decision. Before Richard's key could sound in the front door lock, she finished combing her hair and loosed the top button of her blouse. She smiled at the face in the mirror, mildly amused that the most difficult decision of her life could have clicked into place so suddenly.

She did want a child. She deeply loved her husband, and could see Richard and herself as fine parents. Richard was not one of those men who backed away from responsibility. He was strong and gentle, and he cared for her.

She had put off the decision, she realized, because of the dreams. Now the decision came so easily because after a half hour in the house alone she felt safe from imagined spirits. There had been no new dreams, and Arthur Watson's address was safely gone, a snow of tiny pieces torn and dropped into the trash. Now she and Richard had the entire evening together, and perhaps later, as they curled up for sleep in each other's arms, she would mention that beautiful word.

Chapter 19

At ten-fifteen Monday morning, Meredith eased the car into gear and backed from the narrow parking slot at the Mabton-Grisby Airport. The sky was overcast, but the layer of fog that had settled around Mabton during the night had cleared sufficiently to let Richard's flight leave on schedule. She had stood on the concourse waving at his small face in the cell-like window of the plane. He would return late Wednesday; Thursday, actually, since it would be after midnight when Meredith drove out to meet him.

She accelerated to a leisurely speed on the highway leading back to Mabton, pleased at the possibilities of completely free days. A week ago she might have planned to pick up a newspaper, comb the classified pages, and search for office space. All that had changed now. Her body felt sensuous and satisfied after last night's lovemaking, and a hint of self-satisfaction colored her mood when she thought about her seduction of her husband. She had sat naked under the covers, giving what she thought must be the world's greatest "come hither" smile. "No half shell," she told him. Richard had started to undress. He was half out of his pants, and she thought he was going to kill himself. The pants caught on one foot. Although he was stumbling, he looked like he was dancing. She smiled extra wickedly.

"Honest," she said. "Check in the drawer if you want." She giggled. "Or check in me."

Richard finally managed to get rid of most of his clothes. He moved quickly to her, peeled back the covers, then leaned down and picked her up. "Come on," he said, and stood with her in his arms.

"Wait a minute. It's cold out here," she protested, but Richard paid no attention as he carried her toward the hallway. He would not let her go until they reached the door on the far side. A moment later they stood laughing and shivering in the baby's room, careless of what the neighbors might see through the uncurtained windows. They clung to each other, giggling and deciding a dozen minor details: the baby's birthweight and color of eyes, which college it would attend.

Meredith still felt warm with the laughter of that celebration. She watched the road signs pass and signaled her exit at the one for Mabton State College. No doubt Gus would be too busy to see her; a shame, because she would have liked to reassure him with her good spirits today. The papers lying on the dash had to be returned. She could probably leave them with the secretary.

As she followed the winding road past the campus gate, she noted that the students passing on the gravel walkways no longer looked quite as carefree as they had a week ago. Bundled in warm coats, they hunched over arm loads of books, looking like studious gnomes scurrying between the immense buildings. *Midterms,* Meredith thought, and pulled into a parking space outside the psychology building. She could practically predict the date of major exams by the traces of worry in these faces. She took the thick bundle from the dash, locked the car, and stepped across the lot.

The door to Halburton's office was closed, but inside, his sharp-faced secretary listened on the phone, scribbling numbers on a notepad. Meredith wrote out a brief thank-you note on a scrap of paper and lay the package on the desk. She had almost reached the door, somewhat relieved not to have to discuss the reports with Gus, when a commanding voice stopped her.

"One moment, miss," the secretary snapped, her palm covering the receiver. "You will wait, please."

Meredith paused while the woman put her caller on hold. "You are Miss Morgan, returning doctor's papers?"

"I'm *Mrs*. Morgan," she said. Then she tried to suppress her hostility. *I'm Mrs. Morgan,* she thought sweetly toward the secretary, *and I'm probably pregnant, which is more than you'll ever have going, honey.*

"I'll buzz Doctor."

"There's no appointment," Meredith protested, but the woman had already punched a button.

"Yes," she said into the receiver. "Yes, I caught her. Let me look." The secretary ran a red fingernail down the page of a calendar on her desk. "Well, if you insist, but that meeting . . . All right." She paused, placing her hand over the receiver. "Doctor would like to know if you can see him at eleven forty-five."

"I guess so."

The woman returned to the phone, crossing a line from the calendar to insert Meredith's name. "You may wait here if you like," she said when she set the receiver down. She directed Meredith's attention toward the wide maroon sofa.

Eleven forty-five was nearly an hour away, and Meredith doubted she could endure this woman's company for more than another minute. Nevertheless, curiosity got the best of her. "I didn't plan an appointment. Are you sure there's not some mistake?"

"Doctor wishes to see you. He left instructions." The finality in her voice and the harsh set of her jaw made it clear that Meredith could expect nothing more. She turned without a word and pushed out the office door.

Emerging outside, she wondered what to do with a free hour on campus. Across the grassy quadrangle, where no one sat relaxing today, the broad oak doors of the library swung open and closed as students hurried through them. It was odd for Gus to insist that she come back, and probably for nothing more than to thank her for the dinner, but she supposed she could spend the time reading up on childbirth. That was the only topic that interested her today, and she felt slightly amused as she crossed the open lawn. Babies, nothing but babies, Sally Fielding had said. Well, now she knew how that young wife felt—in some ways, at least. She pulled the heavy library door open, recalling the last time she had been here; a day when she cared about nothing but psychology.

Fifty minutes later, when she recrossed the quadrangle, she felt slightly more knowledgeable about pregnancy. Earlier that morning, studying her face in the mirror, she had frowned in annoyance. It seemed that an act as important as conception should somehow alter a woman's looks, performing a chemical magic to automatically change her physically. Now she acknowledged that the fertilized seed, if in fact they had been lucky, was already making deep, though invisible changes. Her blood chemistry was being subtly altered and a tiny nugget of cells multiplied in her womb. Just in case, she would pick up a package of vitamins with extra calcium and iron. *Just in case,* she thought. So much depended on whether they had gotten lucky.

The door to Gus's office stood open when she entered the waiting room and his secretary waved toward her. "You may go in, miss."

"Gus?" Meredith said tentatively. He sat with his back turned, studying the overcast sky beyond the window and thoughtfully smoking his pipe. "You wanted to see me."

"Meredith, of course. Sit down." He spoke without turning. "But you'll probably want to close the door to the lion's den."

Meredith smiled. Gus's voice sounded serious, but he had not lost his sense of humor. She eased the door to the outer office shut, and by the time she settled into a deep leather chair, he had swung around to face her.

"How are you, Meredith?" His features looked worried. "Forgive an old man for being rude—butting in, perhaps—but I've been concerned about you."

Meredith stared at her lap. She recalled their last conversation here and realized what must be on his mind. "There's nothing to forgive," she said, smiling. "But I think the whole thing has worked out—if you mean about the dreams."

Gus nodded. "That. And your vision. I've been more rude than you think. After I saw you Thursday night, I made a telephone call. A transatlantic call, in fact." He paused to study her reaction. "To England."

Meredith wanted to laugh. At the same time she felt the depth of his concern. "I did look worried last Thursday, but it seems there's no longer anything to worry about." She recalled the bizarre compulsions that tried to lead her to Arthur Watson last Friday. The episode was finished. She really didn't want to think about it. "Don't I look better today?"

She hoped Gus would go for the bait so she could tell him about wanting a baby, but he seemed to miss the comment entirely.

"No dreams?" he asked, his gaze penetrating. "Perhaps I was wrong, then. You do realize that, in a sense, I betrayed our confidence."

Gus had called the British researcher. He explained that he had spoken about the uncanny resemblance of her situation to some things he had heard at the conference. "I dropped those papers by to make sure you would come see me today," he said guilelessly. "I assume you've told none of this to Richard."

"I haven't. I thought I could handle it myself, and I think that's happened."

"Perhaps." Gus remained unconvinced. "In any event, you'll want to know what my colleague in England said."

To refuse would only make him doubt the completeness of her recovery. Meredith nodded.

Gus leaned back and studied the bowl of his pipe. "You read the reports." He cast a critical glance from beneath bushy eyebrows.

"To tell the truth, I found them depressing."

"So did I." He nodded, faintly distracted. "Especially in light of what Dr. Pearlman said at the conference. He did not put all his findings in the papers. He did not mention some bizarre happenings that might be coincidence. He also did not include one family that he met but had no opportunity to study. Not scientifically." Halburton paused, waiting to see if Meredith would prompt him.

"And?"

"This family of four lives in Londonderry." Gus began matter-of-factly laying out the case. "After the mother's death in a car accident the family was thrown into chaos. The mother had been alcoholic and given to blind rages toward the children. She spent a lot of money on her friends at the pubs. Shortly after the funeral, the father and three daughters moved to a cheaper house.

"But the mother followed," Gus said, his usually rich voice reduced to a near whisper. "She first appeared in the father's dreams, much as you have described. She approached him gradually like a lover, recalling pleasant scenes from their life together. She seemed to desire him sexually.

"The man sought psychiatric care, and that brought him to Professor Pearlman. Instead of improving with therapy, the situation got worse."

Meredith wanted to interrupt, to make him stop saying these things, but Halburton's words ran ahead of her.

"The man had three daughters," Gus went on. "He had always wanted a son. In his dreams his wife kept promising a child, the son they never had. The dreams frightened him. Then, before long, he had waking visions like your own. He saw the new house as the old one, his wife present going about her usual chores. You see my point, Meredith. He, too, had three-dimensional hallucinations."

"That could be grief, Gus," she argued. "A man's wife dies, he feels guilty for not helping her with the drinking, he imagines she's haunting him—"

"Except," Gus cut her off sharply, "except for what followed.

"One day, about two years afterward, the man returned to his old house, innocently enough, to pick up some things he had stored there. The new tenant was a young, unmarried woman. In a remarkably short time, he fell in love with her. They married, and the new wife had the long-wanted son. Only after the child was born did she confess to what had attracted her so instantly to her new husband. In dreams, Meredith"—Gus paused, emphasizing the words—"in dreams and visions several weeks before they met, she had seen this same man and fallen in love."

"Gus!" Meredith caught herself, startled at the near shriek in her voice. "I don't want to hear this."

"You must." Halburton leaned forward. "You have to hear, and I only wish I had more records on the family. That might convince us both. They refused to be tested on the equipment, Meredith. They claimed they already knew what had happened and no scientist was going to violate the privacy of their . . . of their . . . how did they put it? Of their miracle."

Meredith felt as if the walls of a trap were closing. She knew what Halburton's next question would be, and she would have to answer it honestly. She stared across the broad desk at the man who had been a friend for so many years. She could not lie to him.

Gus understood. She watched intensity fade from his eyes. His old gentleness returned. When he spoke again his voice was kind.

"I've been abrupt, Meredith, but you can understand why. I had to. In your hallucination, you and the man from your dream talked of having a child. That tallied too well with this Londonderry case. I have to double-check."

Meredith nodded. She was ashamed of her earlier outburst, but she wished she had an excuse to leave.

There was a barbed question that would be coming soon.

Gus went on calmly. "Our relationship is a fine one. We are friends and colleagues, and like all good friends we are counselors to one another. You have always known you could tell me anything or choose not to tell me. That is the choice you must make now, when I ask whether or not the man from your dreams has appeared in your life." As if embarrassed, Gus lowered his gaze and stood to walk slowly toward the far end of the office. He seemed to be staring from the window, but Meredith saw that he was really looking at a small, gold-framed portrait of his wife.

Meredith sat in stunned silence. She wondered if the desperate prayer that filled her mind now could be heard. It asked that none of this be true, that the unearthly bond mysteriously tying her to Arthur Watson be dissolved.

At last Gus's deep voice broke the tension. "That telephone will buzz any minute." He smiled ruefully. "My secretary expects me to attend a twelve-thirty luncheon, and she'll be a terror if I'm late."

"The man has tried to enter my life," Meredith said, "but he's had no luck." Then a really hopeful thought came to her. "He won't have any, either. I'm having a baby, and Richard is the father."

Gus continued to look at the portrait of his wife. "That is very good news," he said. "If we did not have this problem it would be even better news. How has the man entered your life?"

"Actually, it seemed like an accident." Meredith began telling him about the phone call, when Arthur Watson asked to leave items at the yard sale. It was going to be a long story, and the phone was buzzing. Gus answered.

"Two minutes," he said into the phone. He listened and winked at Meredith as the phone seemed to erupt with sound. "Four minutes," he said, and hung up.

"She'll get over it," he said about the secretary. "Still, we have to finish quickly."

"If something, something crazy or supernatural is driving me toward Arthur Watson, it should get discouraged if I'm already pregnant by my husband."

"We can count on nothing," Gus said. "I think for a while you should have someone with you while Richard is at work. I also think that I'd better do some more investigating. Can you find someone? You can always hire one of our students."

"I have friends," Meredith said. "I met some people last Saturday."

"We'll talk very soon," Gus said, lifting his suit jacket from the back of a chair. Meredith was glad that she had not gotten far enough along in her story to tell him about compulsively sitting in a car waiting for Arthur Watson to come home. If Gus knew that he would cancel his lunch. He would cancel his whole afternoon schedule. Somehow the knowledge of that made her feel safer.

"You said there were other bizarre happenings."

"In two cases," Gus said, "there was absolutely insane violence. Dr. Pearlman speculated some force of revenge, but he did so with every caution. He seems to feel that there might be other forces operating." Gus tapped his pipe, then placed it in his jacket pocket. "Undocumented. Even Pearlman was dubious." Gus seemed harassed. He wanted to stay, and had to go.

"I'll take care of myself," she told him. "At least we know what *can* happen. It's not knowing that causes trouble."

* * *

The overcast sky looked darker by the time Meredith stepped from the doorway of the psychology building. Gus had hugged her good-bye. Halburton could not know that his story hung over her as a heavier cloud than she had acknowledged. His tale seemed a dark portent that made all of the crazy events of the last few weeks form a pattern. It was not a rational pattern, but a pattern nonetheless. The pattern said that dead people could return to beg for children, or that strangers' lives could be bound to one another by powers stronger than the bonds of this world.

Dazed, pausing on the steps of the building, she shook her head only to realize that several students were staring at her. They would think she was a patient. She hurried toward her car.

From the distance it appeared that she had gotten a parking ticket. A white rectangle gleamed against the windshield. As she approached, Meredith saw that the rectangle lay not on the windshield, but beneath it. She fumbled in her purse for keys and quickly unlocked the door, puzzled even as her hand closed on the crisp envelope.

Mr. Arthur Watson, the address said in her own handwriting. Dimont Avenue. She let the envelope flutter to the seat, then collapsed beside it. The envelope had been hidden beneath those reports she took to Gus. Richard had not mailed it, had not even seen it. Meredith pulled the car door shut and managed to cover her face with her hands before burning tears broke over her cheeks. The world seemed filled with threat.

Chapter 20

It would never reach him in time. Never.

"Lady, you can mail it or not, whatever you want. I'm only saying I can't guarantee Tuesday delivery."

Meredith blinked and stared across the counter at the impatient face of the postal clerk. She heard his words but couldn't accept their meaning. Arthur Watson would not receive the check in time. She had believed, with the mailing of the check, that the whole business was over and done. But the check had not been mailed.

"Never." She spoke so softly not even she was certain she heard it.

"Beg pardon? Look, ma'am, make up your mind. I got other people waiting."

Meredith picked up the envelope, holding it deliberately away from her body, and turned to file past a row of staring faces. The envelope held nothing but a scrap of paper, worth a few dollars. Yet it felt heavy. This envelope was like cold metal in her hand, the link of a chain that bound her inevitably to Arthur Watson. She had driven all the way downtown to the main depot in hope that mailing it here would guarantee next-day delivery. The clerk's best suggestion had been for her to drop it off at the address. That was one more way of saying *never*—never would this whole business end correctly and well.

She could not risk seeing him. Meredith stepped from the post office and saw that the overcast sky had lowered to become a dancing mist of fog. Her lighthearted mood of the morning seemed to have descended with it and settled as heavily as the clouds. Thoughts of Richard and the hope for a child lay as far away as Richard's return. Too much could happen before then, if Gus's words were true.

"Excuse me, ma'am, coming through."

The door nudged her back and Meredith stepped aside to watch a postal worker push a cart toward a waiting truck. Her car was parked on the far side of the street and she waited for the light to change, wondering what she should do. She could throw the letter away, deliberately misplace it, put it anywhere, but the debt would always be with her, unfinished business in the back of her mind. She crossed the street, opened the car door, and dropped the envelope facedown on the dash. The debt might never be settled, but for now at least she had to get away from it and think. She slammed the car door and locked it before walking away.

It was midafternoon, but heavy clouds cast a layer of dusk down the busy street. Shops had turned on their lights and racks displaying sidewalk sales were being trundled indoors before the mist dampened their contents. The fog itself cloaked the upper stories of the tallest buildings, leaving the pale squares of office windows as faint hallucinations that dissolved and reappeared at changing distances.

Shoppers moved along the damp sidewalks around Meredith, their heads tucked down into packages, their steps certain in the knowledge of where they were going. She dodged them and let the openings set her path, walking idly past store windows that held no interest and hotel doorways where couples laughed, huddling under umbrellas.

Two blocks from the car, she saw a movie marquee glittering through the mist. Bold red letters advertised the name of a famous female lead, above the film's title, *Luck, Love, and New York*. Meredith paused when she reached the theater, studying the posters that lined the building wall. "A love story to warm you all winter" one critic had called it, while another promised, "This is cheer for the grayest day." Above the blurbs stood a picture of a lovely dark-haired girl, dressed in a shimmering glaze of gown, her arm outstretched as she tossed a diamond bracelet toward the background of a ballroom. A remarkably good-looking man in a tuxedo watched, his hand raised to catch the bracelet, while around the two, well-dressed dancers swirled, smiling radiantly.

Meredith did not pause to think. Before she knew it, her hand withdrew two bills from her wallet and pushed them over the counter. She hurried past the ticket taker and into the warm dark of the theater. She wondered what was coming over her. She *never* went to movies in the daytime.

The caverned interior of the theater welcomed her into its subterranean gloom. From the screen, flickering light cast vague illumination over the walls and seats, only a few of which were taken. She slid into one in the center section, relief washing over her. Here she would find peace and time to think, to understand why an unmailed letter could strike such terror into her. Surely by the time the movie ended she would be calm enough to go home.

She slipped her arms from her coat and tucked it around her shoulders, settling into the comfort and privacy of the darkened theater.

The film had already begun. The images flashing in front of her seemed disconnected, confusing at first, but Meredith fought the dreamlike fog filling her mind and gradually sorted out the plot. It turned out to be about a young Iowa girl, the only member of her graduating class ambitious enough to enter a magazine contest. The prize was a weekend trip to New York, where the girl, who had never fit among the plain people of her hometown, blossomed beneath the attention lavished on the contest's winner. She was given clothing and a complete make-over at an elegant salon, then escorted to a formal dance on the arm of a celebrity.

Meredith sat entranced, and a glow of sentimentality carried her deeply into the romance of the movie. Its pastel colors, which would ordinarily appear too sweet, appealed to her today, and even the syrupy music sounded welcome. Dreamlike romance surrounded her. She felt like a princess in a world without dragons or ogres, and the delicate loveliness of the girl made her wish she could be like that: beautiful and wanted.

As it turned out, the good-looking man on the poster had fallen in love with the young Iowa girl, but she did not understand it. The girl mistook his admiration for a sham, one more flattering detail prearranged for the occasion of her winning. She checked out of the hotel early the next morning, ashamed of her own infatuation, and when her escort arrived to take her to the airport he found the room empty.

Meredith tried to discount the fantasy, arguing to herself that it was one more remake of Cinderella, but the fantasy fought back. Deep in her mind it seemed that a different consciousness moved, and that consciousness yearned to believe everything on the screen. It yearned to sink completely into the film's magical world, letting her live in a land like this eternally. As images flickered, the man made a desperate race through the airport. The startled girl was thrilled as she turned back, hearing him shout her name. Meredith could not fight back the tears. They came hot and fast, filling her eyes and spilling onto her cheeks.

Somehow in the midst of the music and the shimmering of crystal chandeliers, she had become that shy Iowa girl. She felt her own willowy awkwardness transformed into sophistication. She felt her plain features enhanced by a beautician's magic until she actually belonged in the film's glittering world. As the lights came up, she burrowed deeper into the seat, embarrassed to be seen with swollen eyes and a tissue still clutched in her hand.

Before long the theater emptied of its few patrons. Meredith gathered her coat and walked slowly up the aisle, passing the trickle of people who had come for the second showing. She had reached the outer doors of the lobby when the theme music struck up at her back, a flurry of orchestral crescendos from the last dance the girl and her escort had shared. Meredith paused. It seemed that her feet actually turned her around, that she had no control over them. A desperate longing to return to that world, to live inside its romance and its swirling passion once more compelled her. She stepped to the refreshment counter, then carried a bag of popcorn and a soft drink inside. Murmurs of happiness seemed to echo in her mind as the pink and blue pastels on the screen showed dawn in an Iowa sky. The least she could do, a voice murmured as she found her old seat in the dark, was to watch the beginning she had missed on the first showing.

Chill wind from a cold sky buffeted her car. Traffic was light. Most people were already home. Fireplaces and furnaces threw heat against the storm of a declining autumn. Leaves blew across the road before the headlights, and it seemed too cold to rain.

It was after ten when Meredith pulled into the driveway, switched off the ignition, and stepped onto the front walk. She had put off leaving the theater, sitting through two more showings of *Luck, Love, and New York* before joining the crowd that flowed toward the exit. Now, as she walked toward her cold house, she hummed the theme. The magical aura of the film floated in her thoughts.

When she first stepped from the theater doors and realized how many hours had passed, the knowledge hit with a wave of cold shock. It seemed impossible that so many hours had gone by, and even more impossible how deeply she had fallen in love with the movie, with the young girl's dreams, and with the beautiful man who arrived to fulfill them. Meredith stopped a moment, leaning against the wall outside the theater, pausing to examine her feelings.

The deepest feeling was shock. She knew that she, or at least her own body, had sat like a tender adolescent in that theater seat for the past seven hours. She knew the film's plot by heart by the middle of the second showing, yet it stirred her emotions again and again. Or else it had stirred someone's emotions, not her own, but feelings that ran along her nerves, made her throat tighten with poignancy, spilled tears from her eyes, and made her shoulders shudder with sobbing that tore through her whole body. How could she have done this? Pregnancy, perhaps. She'd always heard that pregnancy made a woman more emotional, but could such a hormonal reaction sweep over her so quickly? There had to be more to it.

The movie was a release, she supposed, only a pleasant escape from the many fears that had recently been harrying her. That was all. Thankful to have found an explanation, she walked to her car. It was only a release, after all, she decided firmly, and then let her thoughts return to the poignant undertow of emotion the film left in its wake. Its theme song still rang in her ears, and she gave in and let her own heart sway in time with its pull.

She had worried with the girl in the movie over whether what she felt at the dance could be true. She had given up and felt herself a frightened child on a New York street corner, hailing a cab and watching the city slip away through a haze of tears. It was a silly, sentimental movie. Some part of her realized that, but a part of her did not. A part of her absolutely believed such things were still possible.

Meredith slid her key into the front door's lock, recalling the moment that the Iowa girl had entered the rooms of her hotel suite. The door swung inward. Darkness seemed to rush out to greet her. The illusion faded beneath the onslaught of frigid silence from inside the house.

Meredith hurried through the rooms, turning on heat and lights, restless to drive off the gloom. The house had been empty all day and the chilly dampness seemed more present here than it had been outdoors. In fact, the rooms seemed hazed with thin traces of icy fog. She put on a kettle of water and tried to hum the film's theme, but her voice sounded small and frightened in the house's solid silence. She broke off quickly at the kettle's shrill scream and fixed a cup of tea to carry into the living room.

Two magazines had come in the day's mail, and she leafed through the glossy pages, scanning advertisements and photographs. She paused at a home-decorating feature detailing the remodeling of an old house.

A leggy blonde lounged in a rattan chair beside a swimming pool. Sunlight sheeted on the pool's aquamarine surface and struck a diamond of light from the wineglass balanced between the woman's slim fingers. Those fingers lifted as if toasting the photographer at the instant the shutter clicked. Meredith imagined herself inside the same world as that gesture, a world of cashmere and champagne, of limousines and all the soft, expensive furs that the woman must own—sable, otter, mink.

She realized suddenly that she would give anything, anything in this world, to be the woman in the photograph. She had never wanted such a thing before, but now her mind felt captured by want.

If only she had been born into such a world, Meredith thought, she could toss off a gesture as careless and confident. When she closed her eyes and re-created the picture, she could practically smell the delicate, unique scent of her own perfume, a fragrance blended especially for her. It would imprint itself permanently on the collars of those elegant furs, a whispered message to everyone she passed. That message told the world that she belonged among the beautiful, soft surroundings, among cascading fountains and pearlescent marble, among pastel banners of sunsets and gardens and orchids.

Meredith felt her chin drop. She knew she was

dreaming. Or, she said vaguely to herself, *someone* was dreaming. She thought that she should be angry or startled or afraid, but the dream was only a little bit sad. It was pretty in its way, although it was like no dream she had ever had. *Someone* was dreaming.

The dream kept unraveling in shining threads. It spun swirls of molten silver and music, dropped in soft folds like cream poured into a bowl, curved back over itself like the moving silk of surf on a white beach. It wove a cocoon over her senses; a sweet, hushing cloud that enclosed her entirely until she no longer cared if she moved or made a sound.

Arthur Watson's face took shape out of the cloud. He was standing over her, looking down, his eyes wide with concern. His lips moved but his voice sounded thick, as if muffled by the soft fog into which he kept disappearing. His hands reached out of the mist and she shrank from them, calling out after the dazzling dream with its flowery gardens and mossy stones green as gems. Then, all at once, she was lifted up and felt herself fluttering in the air, shaken by her shoulders until her teeth chattered; her head lolled sideways on her shoulder. His hands were gripping her, lifting her up in a fierce and painful grip.

"Don't sit dreaming," his voice seemed to say. "You can't. You can't dream. It won't help. It will only hurt. Please."

The frantic shaking stopped and she stared up at him. His face kept changing. For a moment it was the same, then it disappeared behind the mist to become terrifying; not Arthur's face at all. It was not Arthur. It was the contorted face of another man. Then the fog would fold over him again, and he was Arthur. He was the man she loved, looking down at her with alarm.

"I can't," she heard a small, frightened voice say. "I can't do *that*. I can't do anything. Please let me go."

His fingers loosened and she tore from them, stumbling toward the doorway of the living room. The furniture seemed in all the wrong places, yet she knew it belonged there. A different lamp stood in the hallway, but she flung herself past it without looking, crashing through the half-open door of the bathroom and slamming it shut at her back.

The mirror was not where it belonged. The wall where it ought to be was covered with dappled gray paper. The paper could not be right, yet she remembered putting it there. Arthur had insisted she do something, anything to keep busy, and she had repainted the house. And it was all wrong; dark and icy, the way she felt inside, shades of gray the only thing that made any sense now. All the other colors were frozen, pale and quiet behind layers of ice that shuddered constantly and locked into new patterns inside her. On the dappled gray paper a layer of ice glistened now, growing thicker with each breath she drew. It would wax deeper the longer she watched. It would finally enclose her.

Meredith turned her head to escape the vision. A flicker of movement caught her eye. She looked into the mirror, into the deep surface of reflection in which she would surely drown.

A pale blond woman stared at her from the mirror, her small brown eyes red rimmed and terrified. The woman looked back with the panicked stare of a trapped animal, her cheeks ashen and her shoulders trembling with fear.

Chapter 21

Meredith heard herself scream. The scream was high, coming in two broken bursts. Then it fell silent. Then it rose again, shrilling in measured shrieks. It cut the air like two knife strokes, slashing once, slashing twice. Meredith felt her body tumbling, suddenly turned sideways and sliding on the edge of a soft ridge, like the edge of a couch or a car seat. The two screams rang out again and she grappled with what felt like solid air, trying to push herself up while descending into darkness. She felt her body pressed backward, and the last sensation was of falling into darkness. She was barely aware that her body thumped against something hard.

She awoke feeling pain. She lay on the floor, her arm bruised where it had struck a coffee table when she fell from the couch. A magazine lay where it had dropped. The room was filled with too much light, and the phone was ringing. She gripped the arm of a gray chair and pushed herself to her feet, not knowing whether she was hallucinating or dreaming. Morning light filtered through a slit where gray drapes met. She stumbled toward the kitchen and the ringing phone. Too much time had passed. Had she been unconscious or asleep?

She did not know, and her fear said that it made little difference.

The phone rang again as she reached for it. For no reason she could understand, she placed her hand over the phone and listened without speaking.

"Mrs. Morgan. Hello?"

The voice at the other end of the line made her breathless. It was Arthur, but this could not be a dream. She could see a tree moving in the wind beyond the windows, could hear the sound of traffic passing somewhere nearby.

"Yes?" she said hesitantly. Her voice came out sounding too high pitched, timid, and fearful.

"Mrs. Morgan, this is Arthur, Arthur Watson. Today's mail came and I just wanted you not to worry. The check will come back if you've sent it. I don't yet have a forwarding address."

Meredith's own words cut him off. She spoke those words, feeling her lips move to shape them, yet they were not in her voice. "I'm sorry," she whispered. "Please, Arthur, I'm sorry. I tried, but it isn't my fault. I can't help what happened."

The words tumbled over one another in a breathless rush. Meredith wanted to stop them, but they kept coming, building in layers like the ice in the dream. She wanted to apologize, to reach out to him somehow and make it clear that she loved him. Suddenly, in midsentence, the words stopped. An almost tangible chill issued from the silence at the other end of the line.

No sound came. The line remained open. She heard a harsh intake of breath. Then nothing.

"Arthur?" A voice that was not her own cracked with tension. "Please, say something."

"You are not there," he said at last. Desperation and

fear made his voice tremble. The fear turned to terror. "What number is this? Patty? Who's doing this? Who are you?"

Who is Patty? Meredith wondered, and in the same instant she knew. She was Patty, she herself. But there was another Patty, too. Patty was the name of that woman who had died in the stairwell. Arthur had called her by the name of a dead woman. He had something to do with the woman who killed herself in this house.

The roar of his fear and confusion sounded in Meredith's mind, and she wondered if both of them were going mad. A second later, the dial tone whined, like a whir of insects in the air.

Meredith lowered the receiver to stop the sound. She stared down at it. The phone was black, not the bright red she had chosen. The surface of the table had changed and she knew if she lifted her eyes that the room would also be different. A coat hung over a kitchen chair and she grabbed at it, feeling blindly for the keys in the pocket as she pushed her way out the back door. As she ran toward the garage she heard the phone at her back, ringing, ringing.

Chapter 22

She fled, knowing that she must not answer that phone, hurrying out the door and racing down the drive toward the car. She got it started on the third try, backed out of the drive, and aimed it into the fog that seemed as unreal and crowded with phantoms as her foggy perceptions. A part of her mind realized that Arthur would not call back. It must have been Gus or Richard calling. But suppose it was Arthur? Suppose he once again whispered the name of a woman who was dead?

If Richard were with her the world would become sane. If Gus were with her he would reel out good sense the way he had once reeled computer printouts, even making sense of statistics. Gus would listen to her and nod. He would not understand the possession of one person by the spirit of another. He would listen, though, and account for the fog that swirled and eddied in her mind. He would speak gently, firmly, and she would regain the memory of good sense.

Without Gus, though, her memory faltered from moment to moment. She was driving aimlessly, it seemed, and yet the car felt as if it knew where to turn, where to stop, and finally where to park. Meredith understood that she had driven downtown. At least she found herself back in the car, parked a few blocks from the post office, with the engine cold and reluctant to start. She knew she was wearing the clothes she had worn the day before, and they were rumpled from sleeping in them.

She had slept, she realized. She had pulled the car to a stop in this place some time long ago and fallen back on the seat, exhausted. Now the fog was gone from the lanes of the streets and sunlight shone down into them, but that fog still clung to her thoughts. The world felt cloaked in cotton.

Sometime near midmorning, and long after she had begun to notice strangers staring, she combed her hair carelessly in a restaurant bathroom. The face she found in the mirror was her own, but drawn with exhaustion. More than anything else, that look reassured her. It meant she was still fighting back, even though the battle seemed hopeless.

She could not control what she wanted to do. She knew that she walked along the streets and into stores, but she could not remember why. Moments of lucidity surfaced, startling her into awareness like fixed stars above a chartless ocean. Those moments left memories: a vision of herself standing in the aisle of an expensive department store staring down at a display of perfumes; another vision as she walked past a beautiful mannequin in a shop window and leaned close to the glass to study the delicate features. She had wanted to become that mannequin, permanently fixed in perfection, nearly as much as she had wanted to wear all the perfumes and extravagant clothing she had found in the stores. The yearning was like a tearing inside her heart, as strong as physical pain, yet it could not possibly be fulfilled.

She felt locked in a dream, and if the dream could not come true it was not because she did not completely believe in it. The yearnings could never be fulfilled because the woman who that dream insisted she was, a hopelessly plain and unwanted woman, hardly deserved the attention curious sales clerks paid to her.

Despair was the enemy Meredith fought. Her memory of those hours would surely be lost, but her will, her unquestioning insistence that she deserved to live, remained. The other woman whose frightened eyes startled strangers, whose tiny voice excused herself for standing in anyone's way, might not care if she lived, but Meredith fought back. She willed herself to keep moving, to get through the hours somehow, because sooner or later Richard would come home. None of the hallucinations had been able to last when he was near. Maybe he would even come home early. He was worried about her. She clung to that hope, repeating his name over and over in the depth of her mind.

By midafternoon, Richard's name had become a mumbled, repetitive prayer beneath her thoughts. Then she thought of Gus. She stumbled through traffic to a phone booth. The phone seemed an alien thing, something she must not touch. She willed herself to courage.

"Doctor is in a meeting," the secretary said. "Is this an emergency?"

Meredith gasped, spoke a name, but she could not remember for a moment whether the name had been her own, or if she had said Patty. She replaced the receiver, cutting off the secretary's cold, professional voice.

As afternoon faded, lights winked on in store windows and strangers hurried past. It would be more than a day before Richard's flight arrived, and even if she could wait at the airport she did not have the courage to drive there. The woman who inhabited her now was too terrified to negotiate the complex shuttlings of the highway. She returned to her car and followed a route that crept through side streets to take her home. Her mind rebelled at the idea. Home was the wrong place to go, but compulsion pressed her and there seemed to be no other choice.

Traffic still clogged the main thoroughfares. A circuitous route took nearly an hour to bring her home. By the time the neighborhood grew familiar, Meredith felt exhausted. Each approaching car seemed aimed straight into her headlights, and the thickening fog promised dangers on every side. Her neck hurt from leaning forward to stare through the windshield, but when the Johnsons' house came into view half a block away she eased backward slightly. The Johnsons' house was dark, but in a way that awful house aided her. She began to feel the first stirring of anger. Anger helped. Beyond it lay some deeper emotion, but it felt unrealized, faint as a whisper.

Farther up the street, where a sports car usually stood in the drive, warm light flowed through open curtains. She did not see Sally Fielding's car, but Sally's lights were on.

Gradually, as if struggling upward from sleep, a memory tugged at Meredith. She was supposed to see Sally tonight, but what time? And could she face Sally feeling this way, uncertain from one minute to the next whether she would fade into the woodwork or weep? As she turned into the drive, her relief was tinged with panic, but the panic faltered before anger.

Beyond the windshield the darkened windows of her house offered no welcome. She checked the clock on the dash. It was surely too early, but perhaps she could avoid the gray emptiness inside that house and go directly to Sally's. Meredith pulled her weary body from the car and headed toward the lighted windows.

She rang the bell and heard no movement inside. The open front curtains showed the living room. Meredith was about to turn away when a detail of the furnishings caught her eye. She choked, and found herself weeping.

The walls were patterned with bright blue paper, and a broad orange sofa stood along one wall. The adjacent wall displayed a painting of a ship racing through waves, and beneath it was a polished wood bar with a brass railing around it. Meredith remembered seeing that gleaming bar before, filled with tall bottles and an ice bucket. Now it stood empty.

She had been in this house in her dream. Ed Johnson had been there, too, telling his filthy jokes, and she had fled the people and their voices. She remembered Arthur hurrying her to the door. And the tall red-haired woman, her hair piled high on her head, must have been Sally. The room was lit now, as it had been that night, and the same terror gripped her. Yet this was worse than a dream because it was really happening.

There was some disarray about the room. A young boy's skateboard poked its nose from behind the orange couch. A school satchel lay on the coffee table. Sally had children, and she had taken them somewhere. Meredith's anger returned hesitantly, but the anger was not at Sally. Someone—something—was trying to quell her, maybe even take her life. She tested other emotions. She unconsciously brought her hand to rest on her waist. She knew, suddenly, and without knowing why, that she had conceived. She did not just believe it, she *knew* it. She looked at Sally's living room, at the intelligence and sense of a woman who had said she would not trade her children for a chance to redecorate the White House.

Her steps were loud as she raced from the porch and down the long front walk, the cold air on her cheeks real as a slap. Her anger turned to determination. She could fight back. She *would* fight back. Another life needed her.

All day she had fought the certainty building in her, but now she knew. Drifting between the foggy, dreamlike wandering and lucid moments of awareness, Sally's words had kept echoing. "Poor little thing," Sally had called the young wife. "Shy, timid like a dormouse, walking in like some Hollywood princess." They described perfectly the woman she had seen in the mirror last night. Those words could have come from the lips of any stranger who had seen her today. That timid spirit was trying to possess her completely, and that spirit was going to fail. Meredith suppressed her anger. When you were too angry you could make mistakes.

When she entered her house the attack began, and in spite of her determination it was worse than anything she could have imagined. Visions and dreams drifted. Gray walls were coated with ice. She felt searing, stabbing pain at the sight of the empty house. Arthur was gone. She had tried. She had wanted to love him, had wanted to make love to him. But she could not, and he had given up. He had turned away from her.

She walked aimlessly through her downstairs rooms, hugging her arms against the glacial chill that rolled from the walls. It would not help if she turned up the heat. Nothing could warm the seed of ice that had been planted inside of her. It grew like some monstrous frozen child, swelling huge until it penetrated even her thoughts.

She stared at the dark curtains and saw the endless crevices that hid in each fold. The row of books on the mantel lay like a drift of black snow, and the gray carpet stretched endlessly over the floor, a vast bleak ice field. An extension cord hung from a wall plug, dripping its coils over the ice. She stooped to touch it and it trickled through her fingers like cold water.

She stretched it taut between her hands until it burned her palms. It was strong. It would hold. In her mind she saw the knot it would make over the railing, a dark swelling above the charcoal line of the wood. That knot would yank once, hard, and then the glacier would finally cover her. She stood drawing the plug from the wall, the black cord trailing after her steps across the living room.

She paused at the foot of the stairs and looked up. Above her the harsh geometry of the stairwell spun dizzyingly. Mad angles met diagonal lines and seemed to shift and overlap. They would whirl as she fell. They whirled now as she almost felt herself falling already, gulping freezing air as she passed through it before the cord bit into her neck. The ceiling turned on an unseen axis and she heard a high-pitched, ringing scream in her ears. She tried to cover them, but the sound would not stop. It cut into her like icicles as she stumbled and ran, dragging the cord toward the hall.

The telephone was ringing. Through a haze of confusion and anger Meredith fought her way toward the shrill bursts of sound. Maybe it was Arthur. Maybe Arthur still loved her. Maybe Arthur was calling to save her from death. Her fingers trembled over the phone. She fought against visions. *Maybe Richard was calling*.

"Meredith?"

She gripped the cold receiver, too confused to reply. Who was Meredith? Then she remembered.

"Is Meredith Morgan there?" It was a lilting female voice.

There was a life to protect. She was Meredith Morgan. She told herself that she must never, never forget that. "Yes, I'm here, yes."

"Lordy, you must have been halfway down the block. Sounds like you're getting out of shape."

Meredith suddenly heard the harsh rasping in her throat, her shoulders shuddering as she gasped for breath. "I ran. I had to run to answer. Sally?"

"Sounds like you ran. Yes, it's Sally, and I've got bad news. Mark got tied up on that buying trip. I've got to run some errands for him—I'm dropping off the kids with a sitter and heading downtown to take care of them now. So I guess we'll have to take a rain check for tonight." Sally paused, her voice suddenly uncertain. "Say, are you okay? Say something, will you? Or would you rather just breathe?"

"No. I'm sort of shaky." Breath came in long, clutching spasms. Meredith felt that she would not choke, and she heard her own voice. The timid quaver of the young wife faded. "I had to run for the phone. I was on my way . . ." She trailed off to stare down at the black extension cord—the hanging wire, the wire that could choke and kill—as it emerged from her grip.

"Level with me, kid. Are you alone, or is some raping bastard standing there making you talk?"

"I'm alone, truly I am." The word *rape* wailed through her mind. From somewhere deep in her heart, terror spread like an icy hand. She breathed heavily.

"If you're upset or something, well, hell, I can delay the errands."

"I'll be okay." Some sort of confidence was rising in her. She felt that she had just discovered something important, but did not yet know what it was. The confidence was not very big, but it was there.

"You're sure? I mean, you sound a little bit better, but are you sure you want to be alone tonight?"

Meredith knew what she must do. She somehow understood that if she did not take action now, no one could save her or the child who even now formed inside her. Gus could not. Richard could not, nor could Sally.

"I am sure," she said. "Actually there was someone I needed to see. I won't spend the evening alone."

Sally laughed lightly. "If you put it that way— mysteriously, I mean—I hope it's a man. An old hopeful from college, dreadfully handsome."

Meredith felt insane laughter welling up, but she choked it back before it could spill over into hysteria. "It's not that good, I'm afraid. Good, but not that good." She hung up the phone and felt her confidence rise. Whatever caused death and ice to run through this house seemed willing to allow her to leave, willing that she find Arthur Watson. It even seemed that it wanted her to go.

Chapter 23

The address was more difficult to find because she sought it deliberately. Through the fog, street lights dissolved and reappeared, inscrutable sentinels that seemed to delight in pointing her the wrong way. At last, Meredith found Thirty-second Avenue where it passed near the college. She followed it east, pausing at each intersection to locate the sign for Dimont. Gradually the landmarks became familiar, and she knew she had found the right area when the lighted window of a small delicatessen appeared like a beacon in the fog. She pulled to the curb in front of the red brick building.

Thirty-two-twenty-five Dimont. The man she did not love, but rather the man that the young wife loved, lived here for one more night at least. Meredith took the key from the ignition and leaned against the door wondering exactly how to say what she knew she was going to say. She could think of only two explanations for Arthur's behavior. He had intruded into her life. He had returned on the pretext of selling some things at a yard sale. That could only mean that he was playing games or was himself being compelled by this horror.

She had left her house with no clearly formed plan. In

the instant when she set down the phone she had been
certain of some other realities. She did not love Arthur
Watson, but the young wife had loved him desperately.
It was a love born of that poor woman's emptiness, her
sense of shame for ever having been born. She had
overcome that shame through Arthur's love, but for
some reason his love had failed. In her anguish, facing
unending hopelessness, she had committed suicide.

Gus had tried to explain that, apparently, compulsions
could be guided by dead hands. The dead made demands
on the living. Meredith was ashamed. She had fought the
dreams at every step. Instead, she should have spoken to
Arthur Watson days ago. If she had, tonight's suffering
might have been avoided. She had trusted neither Gus's
instincts, nor her own. That was what it came down to,
simple instinct, and she was trusting her own now.

November darkness descended. Meredith pulled her
collar shut and opened the car door. Clouds of fog
swirled past the streetlamp to give the narrow street a
dreamlike quality, but this was no dream. She felt as
certain of her movements, as if she had performed them
a hundred times. As an afterthought she took the
envelope from the dash and tucked it into her pocket.

The entryway of the apartment building was well lit
and rows of locked mailboxes lined the wall facing the
door. Meredith stepped over to them across the ornate
wine red carpet. It was an old rug, never fine enough to
become an antique, but protected by plastic in the paths
that might have become threadbare, and mended along
one edge where the weave was nearly gone. The mailboxes were polished pink brass, and Meredith caught a
glimpse of her features as she drew her finger across the
row of names. She told herself that she looked like the
back room of a junk shop, but that it was all right. Her

hair might be a mess, and her clothing crumpled, but she was no longer on the defensive. She brushed at her hair with one hand, then decided to forget it. Arthur Watson's name was printed on a small white card beneath the etched figure 2C.

Below his name, a note in small, fine handwriting asked that, beginning tomorrow, mail deliveries be held at the post office for one week until a forwarding address arrived. The date on the note meant he had not yet left, and the handwriting—the neatly inscribed *O*'s and the wide *W* of his last name—stirred a memory. Deep below the semblance of rationality, of purpose, Patty cried out in her mind. This was Arthur's own handwriting and it looked almost too beautiful to contemplate.

Meredith pushed Patty's longing sternly away. The note meant he was still here for one more night, and that was all that mattered.

The carpet leading up from the second landing did not match that in the lobby, but it was just as clean and well mended. She climbed the stairs, studying the fine detail of the woodwork and admiring the years of care that must have been required to bring out its high shine. The brass lamp fixtures were probably the originals, designed for gas, but changed to electric. Lights glowed, casting a safe radiance along the hallway. The door to apartment 2C stood halfway down the hall.

Meredith knocked twice before calling out.

"Arthur? Arthur Watson?" She felt glad to recognize the tones of her own normal voice, free of the wispy uncertainty of Patty's presence. She called again, but there was no reply from inside the locked door.

He had not left yet, Meredith told herself, he was merely out somewhere. She wondered whether she should wait downstairs on the bench in the lobby. He would have to return, but there was no promise it would be soon. Her instinct held firm. She turned and walked back toward the stairs.

Moments later, studying her features once more in the gleaming brass of the mailboxes, Meredith felt her instinct waver for the first time. Her fingers tugged at a corner of the envelope in her coat pocket. Apartment 2C was definitely the right one. Now she noticed a narrow opening at the top of the box. A letter would slide through it, if the envelope were folded. She could discharge the real debt that she owed him and slip away.

The impulse flickered over her mind even as she rejected it. A helpless young suicide's need pressed on her, and it was the most important debt. In addition, she had her own needs. She wanted to lead her own life, not the life of some other woman. She firmly told herself that she would help Patty if she could, but Patty was going to make no more demands. She turned toward the doorway, suddenly sure she should not wait for Arthur to appear. As if the young wife had spoken a message clearly, in that small yet hopeful voice, Meredith knew where she would find Arthur.

The darkness seemed to deepen with the thickening fog. As her steps approached the end of the block, the windows of the Top Stop Tavern glowed before her. Meredith paused beside one to survey the interior before pulling back the door.

Small polished tables stood in a cluster around the low stage. The bandstand was dark, and only half a dozen couples sat scattered through the room. Sitting alone at the bar, his black raincoat folded carefully over a nearby stool, Arthur Watson lifted the page of a newspaper and turned it back. A glass of beer stood untouched before him, and his fine-boned features showed clearly in the mirror behind the bar.

Meredith watched him a moment, attentive to the feelings that whispered in her. She recognized the young wife's yearning, but it seemed pale, a mere flicker of a memory. Her own need was much stronger, a need to understand what they had suffered together. Thankful to be in control, she slid the envelope from her pocket and stepped through the door.

"Mr. Watson," she said, reaching the bar, "excuse me, I don't know if you remember me."

Chapter 24

Arthur Watson looked up from his newspaper. With the first glance, shock and fear clouded his features. Meredith thought for an instant that he would drop the newspaper and run screaming. He made a visible effort to control himself. He smiled thinly.

"Mrs. Morgan. Of course. This is a surprise."

"Not really." Meredith extended the envelope. "To tell the truth, I was looking for you. You weren't home, so I concluded . . ." She paused, realizing what she had been about to say. "I made a lucky guess and found you here."

He took the envelope and stared at it. "Mail? Oh, the check. That really wasn't necessary. I tried to call and say . . ." Meredith watched his cheeks become suddenly pale. She looked away, embarrassed for him.

"Anyway, I got the wrong number," he managed at last.

"My husband meant to mail it and forgot," Meredith went on calmly. Arthur had stood to greet her, but now he eased to his seat again. "I hate loose ends," she said. "It was no trouble." Her lie was obvious. "It *was* some trouble," she admitted, "but it is true that I hate loose ends."

Her words hung in the air as the moment lengthened in uncomfortable silence. Arthur seemed confused. He stared at his newspaper as if he did not recognize how it had gotten there. The tavern had been nearly silent when Meredith entered, but now a couple seated by the jukebox punched a button. The machine whirred and clunked before the opening strains of a country-western tune filled the air.

"Your lady like a drink, Art?" The heavyset bartender looked up from the tiny television at the end of the bar. "Hey, Art, wake up. You've got company."

"Oh, Mrs. Morgan, I'm sorry." Arthur blinked and shook himself from the daze. "Let me buy you a drink. To thank you for the . . . the trouble you took."

"I'd like that. If you call me Meredith."

"Of course."

Meredith felt amazed at her own confidence as she settled onto the barstool. She might have been acting a part in a play, ordering red wine and smiling her thanks when the glass slid into place before her. She was not quite sure how the play would unfold, but an unerring instinct took control of her every movement. She lifted the glass and touched its rim to his. "To your new job. Europe, you said? I guess you're looking forward to going?" It sounded phony, but her instinct told her this was the way to proceed.

Arthur's eyes brightened as he returned the toast. "Actually, I am. Probably for all the wrong reasons." He lowered his gaze. "But let me toast you. You have a new house. To that."

He looked at her, and Meredith took care to study his eyes. They were the same gray-green that had haunted her dreams, but there was a quality in them that the dreams had not portrayed. She had seen it before in the eyes of clients who came to her for help. It was pain; deeply buried and masked by daily pretense, yet honest, deeply felt pain. She followed her instinct.

"Mr. Watson. Arthur. The other day I didn't understand completely, but those things you brought, they seemed so important. And you recognized the new paint in the kitchen. That was your house, wasn't it?"

His shoulders sagged. Now the pain in his eyes mixed with guilt. "That was a stupid deception. I owe you an explanation, but the explanation is incredible. Maybe you would be better off not hearing."

"You don't *owe* me anything," she told him, "but I wonder if we haven't been sharing a problem? If we are sharing a problem, then we probably owe an explanation to ourselves."

He seemed confused. He did not seem evasive, only unable to answer.

"You said you were leaving, maybe for the wrong reasons. Going to Europe may be running away from whatever made you so sad. I wish that day"—she paused, uncomfortable at the memory—"I wish we had been able to talk. Sometimes telling a stranger about unhappiness makes it easier."

His pained gaze studied her for a long moment. Meredith felt that scrutiny probe deeply, asking, trying to know if her kindness was merely idle curiosity. She had felt such study from more than one stranger who had come to her office to talk, and she concentrated now on holding that gaze to reassure him.

At last he spoke. "It's a long and pretty miserable story. Bill over there"—he cocked his head toward the bartender—"Bill hasn't even had to suffer through it, and he's my bartender. The male equivalent of a woman's hairdresser, I guess. Really, Mrs. Morgan, you don't need my trouble."

"I already have your trouble." Meredith looked away to cover the intensity of her words. "What you said the other day, that letting go was harder than you expected, well . . . being *allowed* to let go seems a part of the problem."

"I don't know where to begin." He paused and pushed a strand of hair from his forehead, then cast a rapid glance toward the mirror. The back of his hand lingered, rubbing the small scar over his eyebrow.

Meredith felt her confidence build. The warmth of the small tavern formed a cocoon around them, and Arthur's honesty reassured her. She might have been sitting in her office, faced with the delicate challenge of drawing out a hesitant client. With that thought, her role suddenly became clear, as evident as if a script had magically fallen open to the proper page.

Chapter 25

"Beginnings are always easier if someone asks the right question," Meredith said. She felt rather than saw Arthur's nod as he stared down at his beer glass.

"Did you bring me those things to sell because it was too painful to give them away yourself?"

"I brought them because I *had* to. I didn't want to come anywhere near that house." His voice was low and troubled, but the honesty was clear. "I don't want to spread my trouble around. From any point of view it's madness."

Meredith decided to take a chance. He would either answer or else excuse himself and leave. His honesty would allow no other choice. "Were you compelled by dreams?" she asked. "Did dreams make you come to my house?"

Arthur seemed stunned, unable to speak. His fingers tapped on the bar, and his hands trembled. "Dreams," he whispered.

"Did you dream that you and I were . . . more than strangers?" She had to know the answer. In dreams she had made love to this man all night. She had spent days talking to him as his spirit hovered about her house.

"I had to get away," he whispered. "That's the reason for the job in Europe. Otherwise I'll keep coming back to that house. I know I will. I'll return and return until we are lovers or somebody throws me into an asylum. That's how strong the dreams have been." He was embarrassed, blushing, and even embarrassment could not hide the low tone of terror in his voice. "I've always been a very sane man," he said helplessly. "Up 'til now."

"You'll deal with it. *We'll* deal with it, because we're both sane," she told him. "Something awful has been happening, but it's not because we're crazy. I've also had dreams. You'd best tell me everything about Patty."

Arthur seemed suddenly relieved. He was not inquiring about her dreams, almost as if he did not want to know. He was hesitant but gained confidence. "My wife is, my wife is . . . Patty was a wonderful woman. If you know it was my house, perhaps you know she's dead."

Meredith nodded without explaining how she came by this knowledge.

"Dead. First time I've actually said it. It seems so final, like letting go of those things last week."

"You loved your wife, Patty, very much?"

"Not enough." The words were harsh, and a rocklike hardening of the cords in his neck nearly squelched his voice. He cast a sideways glance too quick to betray its meaning. "She committed suicide. It was my fault, and it wasn't. I told you, it's a long, miserable story."

Meredith allowed the silence to lengthen, her hand trembling as it touched the stem of her wineglass. She took a sip. "Was it completely unexpected? Even now, you seem in shock."

"Not completely. I should have guessed, should have done better. You see, Patty wasn't as strong as most people. Her parents died in a car accident when she was young. She grew up being told it was her fault."

Beneath the fabric of his shirt, a shudder tightened the contoured muscles of his back and shoulders. He suppressed it. "They were on their way to pick her up at her grandmother's house. The grandmother had been baby-sitting. They were late, maybe driving too fast, maybe drinking. At any rate, after they died the grandmother raised Patty."

Meredith listened without interrupting his troubled words. Occasionally words would fail him, trailing off in a sign of frustration, and she would prompt him gently, probing further with brief questions to let him know she was still listening and that she cared. Arthur spoke in a monotone without looking at her. The story he told felt oddly familiar, as if she had lived through it a long time ago, herself the seven-year-old child consigned to the care of a resentful grandmother, punished daily with blame. "She was told that if she had *wanted* to stay with her grandmother overnight, her parents would not have been driving to pick her up," Arthur said softly. "And that she was to blame for their deaths."

By the time Patty entered a private high school, Arthur explained, she was barely able to look her classmates in the eyes. A jittery bundle of frayed fears and self-hatred, she would panic if she heard a door slam.

"Did you meet her there? Were you both in private school?"

"We met at the movies."

Patty had loved movies, he said. "And I was an up-and-coming usher for matinees after school." He smiled slightly and sipped his beer. "She always sat in the back. Didn't want to block anyone else's view."

Arthur had watched the shy, star-struck girl for three

weeks before he spoke. He saw a fragile, beautiful child, avoiding his eyes as she hurried into the theater, curling up in her seat to become lost in wonder at the fabulous images spread out on the screen. Then one day, searching for words to get her attention as she left the theater, he managed to stammer out that she looked like the star in the film.

"I felt dumb the minute it came out. Typical teenage come-on, huh? But I couldn't believe how she took it. Like I was the sun and she could unfold like a flower. It didn't happen all at once, of course, but she sort of smiled that day. Before she got out the door, I found out her name."

Arthur had coaxed her, in the weeks that followed, into going out for walks after the movies. Supposedly they were taking her home, but Patty never wanted to arrive there. They would dawdle, staring into shop windows and strolling through department store furniture displays, pretending the place was a huge house that they lived in. Together they would fill out the fantasies; they would be rich and have servants to wait on them, they would have heaps of children, each with rooms of their own, and a place in the country with animals. Then one day Arthur got scared. They were both about to graduate and he would go to college, but he knew he wanted to marry this delicate, whimsical girl who was so unlike the loud, pushy girls at school. But what if Patty really did want the dreams they talked about? He figured he would go to college, graduate, and get a good job, but doubted that he would ever be rich. Even good salaries did not pay for their kind of dreams.

"So I asked, straight out, would it have to be like that, swimming pools and cars and long vacations everyplace the sun was shining. Could she live without that?"

"And?"

"Patty said none of that mattered, except for the children. At which point I proposed."

Strained lines in Arthur's face seemed to soften gradually as he poured out the memory. Now he glanced toward Meredith's glass. Like his own, it was empty. "Like another?"

Meredith nodded. "Actually, she sounds very special. I can see why you loved her."

Arthur trembled, hearing the words in the past tense. He turned and signaled to the bartender. When the drinks arrived, Meredith asked, "So you got married?"

Arthur nodded. "My parents paid for a wonderful honeymoon. We went to a lake."

Meredith interrupted, fearful of the memory the words stirred in her. "And you went to college?"

"College? Yes. Patty seemed stronger in those days. She had a job."

They had lived in a small apartment while he attended classes, his wife working days as a cashier. Scholarships and study through summers let him finish in three years.

"Patty was ecstatic when I got a good job. We bought a house." Arthur paused. "That house where you live. She quit her job and we began planning for the way we always wanted to live. Patty wanted children right away; we both did. Patty would read books about raising kids and talk to the neighbors, at least one." He broke off suddenly and pressed his lips tight, straining for control. His eyes glittered. "Maybe you know Elsa Johnson?"

"Unfortunately," Meredith said, offering a grim smile. "For someone like Patty, Elsa would not be easy to take."

"I wish it had been so simple." Arthur's voice was harsh with resignation. "Elsa was one of Patty's few friends, if you can call her a friend. Patty wanted kids and Elsa would get her talking on that. I wasn't home all day. We needed extra money, planning for a family. I coached basketball in the evenings at the high school. Maybe that was wrong." Arthur's voice faltered and he turned his head away before going on. "I sound like I'm making excuses, but I loved her. We wanted so much for the child. . . . She thought she was pregnant. I should have been there that night."

He was blaming himself for something, but Meredith could not quite understand. She searched her memory, trying to discover what had happened. His wife had not died at night—Sally said it was during the day. Elsa had found her. And Arthur had said nothing about the house being gray, about Patty's collapse into what had to be madness. Was he deliberately leaving out part of the story?

At her side, Arthur smoothed a finger over and over the scar on his forehead. He was not lying, only terribly sad. He sat silent.

"When I moved in, the house was, well, pretty depressing," she said. "Was it always that way?"

"No." Arthur seemed to have come to a decision to go on. "That was afterward. After what happened. Anyway, I was coaching and one night I got home pretty late. I figured Patty would tease me, kidding around that she was beginning to believe Elsa. Elsa kept insisting that I had another woman. Patty never believed it—not then. Elsa could be so cruel, damn her."

He paused a moment to calm himself. Patty had not been home, he explained. A note told him she'd run to the grocery store. She took the car but it was only a few blocks' walk. When he got there, the car was parked in the lot. He went into the store to catch up with her but she was gone. The clerk said she ought to be home by then.

Meredith felt a chill pass over her skin. The memory felt familiar, but not like the others she had known. This was darker, filled with violence and terror, an inky pool in the depth of her mind. This was a place where even the young wife had not dared lead her.

"She was in the car." Meredith breathed the words, unsure they were audible. "You . . . found . . ." She closed her eyes against the thought that Arthur's words would not shut out.

"Rape. He was all over her. A big son of a bitch with a rubber Halloween mask. I don't know who or what he was, only the smell of whiskey. I pulled him onto the pavement but he had a knife."

"Your scar?"

"That and a couple of others. Nothing serious. I was too late, Meredith. Poor Patty, beaten up and lying there too frightened to move; me with blood across my face like I'd been murdered. We didn't even call the police, just got the hell out of there."

Meredith listened, and one by one the gaps in her memory filled. She saw the man who sat by her now as he had been that night. He had tried to comfort his wife, drive her home, get her into clean clothes and to bed. But neither of them could sleep. They had lain awake, her form frozen beside him in stony silence. He tried to get her to talk, but she merely stared back helplessly. When they finally fell asleep, he moved close to her during the night and she woke up screaming.

"I don't think Patty always knew after that. I mean whether I loved her, even who I was all the time. I tried to talk to her about it, and tried not to talk about it, to distract her, to leave her alone."

"Nothing worked?"

"Nothing," Arthur echoed. "I wanted to get her help, but just going out of the house terrified her. She would say no, pretending to be too busy or tired, but we both knew. I kept telling myself how she had been back when we met. If she could come out of that, I would bring her out of this somehow."

He had thought that changing the house, those rooms where she spent all day alone, might help. Patty insisted on doing the work herself. She was afraid, he realized now, of having anyone else around. At first he thought the gray paint was only for trim, but gradually it had covered the walls and ceilings. Patty argued when he objected to it.

"In a way I guess it was a dumb idea, but I thought letting her do that might make up for the crying. She never cried, at least not in front of me. She would freeze up if I tried to talk about what happened. I thought maybe by painting the house gray, she could see, outside her mind, what her feelings were like. Maybe she could recognize them when they were on the outside." He paused and looked toward Meredith with a helpless shrug. "Does that make any sense?"

"Not logically, but emotionally it does. At least it was a place to start expressing what she felt."

Meredith turned the memories over and over in her mind. She saw a young woman wanting a child, yet afraid of her own husband's touch, unsure what love was anymore, not even able to cry. Then those terrible gray walls, her one attempt to deal with her feelings. It was too ugly to contemplate, but it had happened. In her mind's eye, she saw Patty, trapped in the prison she had created, dozing off into dreams of movie stars and gleaming limousines. It was an escape, but Arthur no longer shared it. She had been so alone, it was no wonder.

"So the feelings, that house, finally became too much," she said quietly.

She studied the slender, sensitive man at her side. His face was etched with exhaustion and pain. It had been months since Patty's death, but he had lived that day over and over, blaming himself because he had been gone that night, because he had not found help or been strong enough to pull her through and back to reality.

Arthur shook his head slowly, but did not answer. Instead he spread his hands open on the polished bar. Meredith saw the wide gold band on his ring finger.

"I put it back on today," he said, lifting the hand and letting it fall. "I know she's gone, but it doesn't seem to make any difference. I dream about her. Sometimes I'll see a woman hesitate before crossing a street, and I think it's Patty. Or hear a voice. That wrong number today."

Meredith wanted to speak, and knew now that he could probably understand how her entire being had been taken over by whatever dwelt in that house. At the same time, it might make him more fearful. It might make him feel more guilty, as if he were to blame for what had happened to her.

A sudden movement saved her from having to decide whether to tell him. Arthur stared into the mirror behind the bar, then stood. "We have to go. Let's walk." He turned to the bartender. "We're using the back door, Bill."

The bartender looked up from the television. He grunted. Grinned.

"I don't mind a walk . . . ," she began. Arthur's hand held her elbow, and he steered her through a back room stacked with beer cases. "What's wrong?" she said. "What's happening?"

They stepped into an alley. He led her along the alley back to the street.

"Sorry." Arthur's grip loosened. "He came past the window and I figured you didn't need that." The night was getting chilly, but he trembled with more than cold. Anger made his voice like ice.

"Need what?" Meredith stared in amazement. His arm encircled her protectively.

"I thought you saw." Arthur's arm pushed her gently toward the tavern's window. "Take a look."

The lower part of the window was steamy with fog, but over the hazy ridge she saw a bulky-looking man take a seat at the bar. Then Meredith saw his face.

"Ed Johnson," she said, startled. "Elsa's husband."

"He came past the window, and he's come before," Arthur said bitterly. "Someday, somebody will hit him between the eyes with a hammer." Arthur looked up and down the street. "He's most likely here to meet some woman."

"How much does Elsa know?" Meredith whispered.

Arthur stood in the mist and tried to control his anger. "You're new in that neighborhood. Hasn't anyone there tipped you off?"

"I haven't met many people." She stood, trying to remember what Sally had told her about the Johnsons.

"It's a perverse game," Arthur said. "Elsa lets Ed date any woman who can stand him, and Ed covers the town as Elsa's reporter. It isn't that big a town." He continued to look through the window at Ed Johnson. "No marriage is safe with those two around, including yours. I don't know how he suspected you were here. Maybe he doesn't suspect. This is one of his regular stops."

"Spying."

"You can bet your life on it." Arthur's fury caused him to whisper his hatred. "He spies on everybody."

He was so troubled that he sagged against the wall of the building. "I was with a woman. The only time I was ever with another woman. I've always suspected that Elsa told Patty, but I never asked. Patty couldn't have stood that kind of bluntness, and I didn't want to know. Maybe I had no right."

Meredith felt the knowledge slip gently into place, like the last tumbler releasing a lock. The door of her memory opened. Arthur could not know, but she did. Elsa had told Patty and had killed her as surely as if she had knotted the noose. And Elsa knew it, too. It was vicious, evil, more cruel than even Meredith could believe.

She said nothing, thankful she had not tried to explain all she knew. She had felt only Patty's feelings, never Arthur's. Whatever he had done, there had to be a reason. She turned to study the profile outlined dimly in the fog. Arthur stood like a condemned man.

"You blame yourself for seeing another woman," she said flatly. "Patty, all those months you could not touch her, feel her love."

"It wasn't love." Harsh words cut her off. "What I did. Call it desperation. Call it lust. Cunning. I even rented a room where I could be alone a few hours a day. Then I met a woman. I took her to that room. Once. But what it amounted to was that I turned from Patty when she needed me most."

"What did *you* need?" Meredith tried to force perspective on him. "Escape? What else? Walls that weren't gray, and arms that weren't closed against you?"

"It can't be forgiven." Arthur's voice was so filled with pain that he could hardly speak.

"I can forgive it, if you can't," she said. "Whether you can forgive yourself or not, at least we can get past what is harming us. It's scary, but not as bad as living the way you've been living." She thought of her own problems. "I have to live in that house. We have to get this situation fixed so I can do that."

He was so filled with guilt and anger that he seemed not to hear.

"I have a plan," she told him. Not only had the tumblers of the lock clicked, but now a door seemed open. She felt nearly able to predict events. Meredith knew what she must do. "I'll need your help and every bit of luck we can get hold of."

Chapter 26

They stood in the fog and darkness outside the bar. Meredith believed she understood more than she would ever tell Arthur Watson. There was a spirit of evil in her house, but an evil that rose from despair. As a counselor, Meredith had seen plenty of intimidated, unhappy people. She understood what drove Patty to suicide. She understood how Patty blamed herself for losing Arthur, and how Patty, even as a very young girl, had learned to suppress her anger beneath timidity.

And yet Patty had every right to be angry. In fact, she had every right to be *furious*. She had been raised by a narrow and probably stupid grandmother. She had her dreams obliterated by rape. She had suffered Elsa's vicious tongue. It was no wonder that a spirit of violence lived in that house, along with Patty's spirit of meekness.

"We're going to go back into the bar," Meredith told Arthur. "Pretend that we've just arrived. When Ed Johnson sees us, just act as if we don't care. We'll take a booth close enough that he can hear."

"Is this wise?" Arthur asked. "And don't worry, that son of a bitch will hear us." He looked at Meredith, and there was both tenderness and protectiveness in his eyes. She could understand why Patty had loved him.

"I need you to do two things," she said. "When I start raising my voice, you sit quietly. I'll pretend to be angry. I'll really be acting pretty badly. When I storm out of there, please call this phone number. A man named Gus will answer." She fumbled in her purse and found a ballpoint. "Give me that envelope."

Arthur passed her the envelope containing the check. She wrote Gus's home phone number. "When Gus answers," she said, "tell him what is happening. Ask him to get over to my house right away."

Arthur stared through the window and seemed unable to believe that they were going back into the bar. He watched Ed Johnson. Anger tightened Arthur's lips. The scar was white, like a streak of bleach on red cloth. His fists clenched.

"After you call Gus," Meredith said, "I want you to wait until Ed leaves. The minute he leaves, come to the house—fast. Come in the front door. . . ." She fumbled in her purse again. "Here's the key to the front door."

Arthur Watson stood confused, but obviously willing. Meredith knew she could not explain everything she planned.

Instinct guided her. Instinct told her who had raped Patty. She was sure she knew who had been causing what Elsa called "incidents" in the neighborhood. She wondered if Elsa also knew.

But she could not tell Arthur. If Arthur understood that Ed Johnson was the rapist, Arthur might walk in there and kill him. Ed and Elsa Johnson had destroyed Patty. She would not allow them to destroy Arthur.

"Act casual," she told Arthur. "You don't have to be nice to him. Just pretend that you don't care."

As they entered, Ed Johnson turned on his barstool.

He took a quick gulp at his whiskey and water, grinned, and jumped to his feet like a welcoming committee. "It's old Art," he said, "and damn if I can believe who's with him." Ed's face was reddened from drinking, but he moved accurately. He had not been drinking for very long. He advanced toward Meredith, arms out, as if to give her a hug.

Meredith thought of Sally and how Sally had dealt with Ed. Sally cussed whenever she wanted, and it seemed to work. Meredith dodged the encircling arm. "Stick it, Ed," she told him, "where the sun don't shine." She forced herself to giggle.

Arthur was about to be a problem. His anger was so intense she was afraid he would take action. She could not have him getting into a fight. She took his arm, trying to lead him to a booth.

"Get this," Arthur told Ed, "and get it good. Stay away from this woman. Go phone that old bat you're married to. Spread the news. Do whatever crap you have to do, but stay away."

Ed Johnson ignored Arthur. He looked at Meredith. "You've got some things to learn, little lady. This simp won't teach you much." He turned his back on Arthur, his movement filled with contempt.

"Take it easy," she whispered to Arthur. "Head for a booth."

From start to finish it took half an hour. Meredith watched the clock as she and Arthur whispered, fresh drinks untouched in front of them. Ed sat at the bar listening. He could not hear their whispers, but he was not about to move.

"Talk about anything," Meredith told Arthur. "Tell stories. Talk about the weather. It makes no difference, but just keep whispering for now." She watched the clock. After a half hour, when the clock read eight, she bumped her knee against Arthur's knee. "I'm going into my act," she said. "I'm going to act just awful. Don't say anything. Just call Gus when Ed leaves, then get over to the house."

She was not an actress, and she had never even liked movies all that much. Now some invisible will seemed to aid her. She pretended to herself that Arthur had just made a proposition. She pretended that she felt guilty toward Richard because she was out with another man. She pretended that she was afraid, because Ed Johnson would tell the whole town that she was having an affair. The pretending worked.

She pushed her wineglass away, so abruptly that it clicked against the side of the booth. Wine slopped on the table as she stood. "You bastard," she said to Arthur in a voice loud enough for Ed to hear. "You seamy bastard."

Arthur sat looking confused. She figured it was not hard for him to do, because he didn't know what was going on.

"Before I'd do *that*," she said, "I'd spend the rest of my life in a convent. I thought you were a nice guy." She stood, fumbling in her purse, and threw ten dollars on the table. "I won't even let you say you paid for drinks," she told him. "Richard may be out of town, but I'll spend the night alone—alone, dammit—before I put up with you." She put on her coat, pretending difficulty getting an arm into a sleeve. When she walked from the bar she pretended to nearly lose her balance. Behind her, Arthur sat like a man who had just been clubbed. Ed Johnson perched on his barstool, and his ugly grin showed below a gaze that undressed her as she passed him. By the time she opened the door Ed was already headed for the phone.

Fog swirled in darkness, and the neon sign of the Top Stop Tavern glowed like a red eye behind her as she walked to her car. Meredith knew she was in a desperate game, but it seemed to her she had no choice. Part of her anger was real, and she knew she had to put it to rest. If she did not get rid of her anger, there was no telling what would happen when she got home.

She was angry at Patty, or at least she was angry at the sobbing and sad and sometimes vengeful force that lived in her house. Patty was dead, but an evil force existed. She did not know how much Arthur understood, but she knew what Patty wanted. She knew that Patty had wanted her to bear Arthur's child, the child that Patty did not have.

Maybe, she told herself, maybe it was the last way that Patty had to show Arthur how much she had loved him. Maybe it was something worse. Maybe the evil that had been done now ruled Patty's spirit.

If that was true, then the real enemy was the evil that living people had caused. A rapist and his filthy-mouthed wife had caused more evil than anything that could come out of some invisible world of terror. She told herself that Patty had been a victim, and Patty was *still* a victim. That might or might not be true, but it helped her lay aside her anger.

She wanted a few minutes at home before Ed Johnson showed up, so she drove as rapidly as safety would allow. She had no doubt that the man would fall for the bait. She was an attractive woman who had just announced that she would spend the night alone.

Rape. Even the thought thrust a fear into her that was

more terrible than her memory of gray walls. She thought of the vision within those walls, the vision of a woman screaming. She thought of the brutality and violence of men like Ed.

Except, she told herself, Ed's kind were not men. Arthur and Richard were men, but Ed was not. There was not much she could say or do about such swine, but she could do something about one of them. Meredith told herself that before this night was over, Ed Johnson was headed either for prison or for hell. That would give Elsa a tasty piece of gossip.

Chapter 27

Elsa's house was dark as Meredith passed, except for the blue light of a television that flickered in the windows. The street was dark because the street lights were engulfed by fog. Her own house stood shrouded in that mist. Fingers of it, and fingers of cold, brushed around her as she parked the car and walked to the back door.

She figured that she did not have much time, but still she hesitated before opening the door. She wondered how many people had lived in this house before her and wondered how many hopes and dreams had been born or died here. All she could truly say was that this house had seen the death of a young woman's dreams and the beginning of her own dreams for a child. It had seen two good men, Arthur and Richard, doing their best. As she turned the lock she promised herself a future that would redeem the sadness from this place. She told herself that, as a counselor, her business was to assist those in trouble. Was the human spirit any less deserving just because it was wrapped in the hideous clutches of invisibility and death?

She also told herself that she was prepared for anything when she opened that door. She was prepared for gray walls, for the sobbing decay of dreams, even for an icy force that pressed her toward suicide. Meredith knew she was no longer vulnerable. She thought she had seen all there was to know about the dark heart of the house. Yet when she opened the door she was momentarily stunned by the feelings that lay in wait throughout the rooms.

A nearly overwhelming aura of loveliness seemed to echo in each dark corner. For a few moments she did not even switch on lights because she was so compelled by an air of happiness and hope. The feelings were quiet, but they were true. When she switched on the light the walls were not gray. Nor were they the colors she had painted them.

The paint seemed new. Tidily ironed curtains hung over fog-shrouded windows. Furniture had obviously been bought secondhand, but it shone with polish. From the living room came low strains from an old-fashioned record player. The music came from Broadway shows. The kitchen showed small personal touches; a recipe held to the refrigerator by a magnet, a couple of blooming plants, a worn tablecloth that was clean and ironed. She walked through the living room, made cozy with a plaid sofa and maple end tables. Hand-me-down lace with tattered edges protected the surface of one, and condensation gathered on the shining surface of a bowl of flowers. The feelings of loveliness combined with feelings of hope. This was a house that was deeply loved, a place to live in, a place to bring children.

Steeling her mind against the meaning of what she must do, she gripped the polished brass of the front door and pressed her thumb on the latch to click the lock open. She feared what might come through that door soon, but she did not want the spirit of this house to know it yet. She eased the door open to be sure it would be ready, and a scrap of paper taped to the brass knocker caught her eye.

It was a note on creamy white stationery. Signed simply, "Sally." Meredith skimmed it quickly in the dim light. "Sorry I missed you, but give me a ring when you get in. I got a call from someone special—be ready for a sexy hunk to come through the door tonight!"

Meredith shuddered. Sally could not know what might happen here tonight. It was a sick joke, perhaps even Elsa had pulled it. Her fingers snapped open, as if the scrap of paper had ignited in her grasp, and it fluttered to the stone floor of the porch. She shut the door, but left the lock unlatched.

Turning back, she paused to study the living room again. For the first time, she noticed the silver-framed picture on the mantel. Patty had not been a plain woman, she saw when she approached it. Patty only thought she was plain. Patty was truly beautiful standing beside the tall and gentle figure of Arthur Watson. She gazed up at him as he touched her cheek with one finger, and that touch looked even lighter, even softer than the white gauze of a wedding veil, which still billowed from the turning of Patty's head.

Meredith stood stunned. *This* was the way the house had been before the rape. *This* was what had been stolen from Patty. Meredith was unable to move, and tears came to her eyes as she thought of the young wife lovingly and carefully putting together her home. There could be no crime greater than the destruction of dreams.

"I don't know anything about the invisible world," she said aloud into the emptiness of the house. "I do know about right and wrong. It's right for me to give an explanation. Something ugly is about to happen here, but it's not as ugly as what has already happened." She paused, wondering if she was doing the right thing. At the same time she knew it was the only thing she could do.

She walked through the empty rooms. She knew she should hurry, because surely Ed would show up very soon. At the same time she had to make her own peace with the torn spirits of this house. If Patty was actually here—if the harmed presence of Patty was trapped in this place and unable to leave—then that spirit deserved her attention. The aura of love and hope surrounded her and did not diminish. The very least she could do was respect what had once given life to this house.

"There was never a moment when Arthur Watson did not love his wife," she said to the empty rooms. "Let me explain."

She walked through the house murmuring her explanations. Since she knew nothing about the world of spirits she told everything she knew; about Arthur, about herself and Richard, about her own hopes. She told Patty, and as she spoke the words she knew they were true, that she was going to have a child in this house. She promised that the room upstairs would belong to that child and that they would always keep it safe. She talked to the house as if the house itself were Patty. She talked to Patty in the way she might talk to Sally, or at least the way she would talk to Sally when they became better friends.

As she talked she felt the rise of a timid companionship. There was a presence here, and it was becoming stronger. From what she knew of Patty the presence should have been apologetic, but this presence was not. It seemed contained within a greater presence, as if Patty were trapped by the evil that had been done to her. The presence seemed in suspension, granting Meredith full freedom to move about and talk. At the same time, she felt an enormous power. That power might be dark. She would be frightened into immobility if it became manifest.

"There is no reason for you to feel guilty about anything," Meredith said. "I do not know what rules bind you, but you have done your best. Now I'll do my best. I have something to say that you have to know."

She did not want to tell about Ed Johnson, but Ed was the root of sorrow in this house and she felt she must. As she walked through the rooms and began speaking of Ed, the aura of happiness fled like running water. Emptiness seemed to lie all around her, and she felt the presence as a glowering, barely constrained force. It was getting stronger. Fresh paint seemed not so fresh. The rooms lost their feeling of hope and beauty. Low sobbing spread through the house, and Meredith did not know whether the sobbing came from the house or from herself. She was so engrossed in what she had to do that she did not hear the muffled footsteps outside the door. Instead, she was suddenly transfixed. From the living room came a terrified scream, a scream muffled by time and sorrow.

Chapter 28

Meredith could not move for what seemed like minutes or hours. Forms in the house shifted, and the paint faded, changing to a light sheen of gray. The force seemed to gather, ominous and brooding. At the same time it did not seem threatening, at least not to her. That gave her confidence.

When she did move, walking hesitantly through the living room and toward the kitchen, it was with the nearly serene knowledge that even the house itself was protecting her. She told herself that she was safe and that she had planned this. She told herself that Arthur and Gus were probably outside the front door right now.

Everything she told herself made no difference, at least momentarily. Huge and slightly weaving his way in through the door, Ed Johnson stood. He was always a big man, and now he seemed enormous. His fleshy face radiated animal delight, like a dog given a new bone. He was at ease, and that was the most frightening thing. His huge hands rested on his hips, as he surveyed the dining room, then looked at Meredith. He hitched his belt over a belly going to fat, and he tapped his belt buckle as he winked.

Meredith's scream matched those rising from the living room.

"You got yourself a problem, little darlin'," he told her. "But I expect your neighbor Ed can fix it."

He was big and drunk and strong and he would hurt her. Meredith backed away as screams rose like a dying voice from the living room. Ed came forward slowly, and he either did not hear the screams or did not care. She had not expected him to be so obvious, and she moved around the dining room table. It made a poor object to hide behind, but the reaction was automatic.

"You can't get away with this," she said. "You've got to be crazy. You're not even trying to hide who you are."

"You won't say anything," he told her. "You won't say anything because you don't want your old man to know about Art Watson. If you'll screw around with one guy, you'll screw around with two."

Then Ed's voice lowered and he stopped. He was taking pleasure from the game, taking his time, prolonging her fear. He stood trying to wipe a grin from his face, trying to make his voice sound gentle. "I'm not gonna hurt you. You'll like it." He could not help chuckling. "In fact, if you think a wimp like Art is good, you'll *love* this." He moved again, his movements slow and deliberate. He seemed to be taking satisfaction from the knowledge of his power. He seemed to be telling her that no matter what she did, he was in control and she was helpless.

"Elsa isn't going to love it," she said grimly. After the initial shock, and confident that Arthur and Gus were near, her courage was returning. Behind Ed's back she saw the gray walls darkening, and she felt the cold chill of grayness and ice. The house was saturated with cold as the walls went from dark gray to black.

"Elsa *is* gonna love it," he said. "You don't know my

old sweetie like I do. Call her up. She'll come sell tickets."

"I shouldn't tell you this," Meredith said. "I ought to let you go ahead and hang yourself, but I'll give you a fair warning. We are not alone. If you keep this up you'll be caught."

"If you're going to fool around with guys," he said, "you're going to have to lie better than that." Now his voice deepened with intent. He flexed his hands, watching her, waiting for her to run. "It's more fun for you if you cooperate. For myself, I like it either way."

No one was coming to help her. At least not yet. Meredith was confused. She had told Arthur to come in the front door. He had the key in case Ed had locked it. Yet the only presences in the living room were coldness and ice.

She fought terror. If Ed grabbed her she would shrivel from the very filth of his touch. What was keeping Arthur? Had he driven too fast and had an accident? A hundred possibilities for delay shot through her mind. She had made an awful mistake. Maybe Arthur was not coming.

Ed slowly moved around the table, but he stayed between her and the door to the kitchen. His body seemed massive, and an amused leer cut creases into his face. "You could make a break for the living room," he chuckled. "See if you can get to the front door. I'll show you all about an open field tackle."

He would not only harm her. He would make her lose the baby. He would maul her; make her body into something detestable. Arthur was not coming. Meredith felt chill from the house as icy wind spread outward from frozen walls.

"I got time," Ed told her. "We can chase around this

table half the night. I kind of get a kick out of it." He reached across the table, and Meredith nearly fell as she stumbled backward.

"You're gonna have to be quicker than that." Ed held a huge hand before him, and it seemed to her like the head of a snake about to strike.

Something had gone wrong. There was going to be no help. She had been a fool to set up this plan. Meredith gauged the distance to the kitchen, then edged around the table. If she could just get him to move a foot farther to the left she might have a chance to get through the back doorway.

"Give it up, little darlin'. You're cornered." Ed would not move far enough to the left. He moved only a little. He was trying to make her believe that she had enough room to flee. Meredith looked toward the kitchen, wondering if she should take a chance.

A confusion of shadows lay across the kitchen floor. There seemed to be some kind of silent struggle going on in the kitchen. There was more than one person there. Not a sound, but someone was in her house, just out of the line of vision. Meredith was confused. She had told Arthur to come in the front door.

Whoever was there could be anyone. It could be a prowler. On the other hand, whoever was there could be no worse than Ed Johnson.

"You have no right to break into my house," she told Ed. "If you so much as touch me you've committed a bigger crime. Go away."

She had to keep him talking. "You tried to rape that schoolgirl at the grocery store," she said. "You raped the woman of this house. You've done it to other women."

"Sweet little Patty," Ed said, and now he started moving quickly. "She was tough. You wouldn't think a bitch that little could fight that hard." He reached across the table and brushed Meredith's arm. She jumped back. "Give it up," Ed told her. "I don't want to have to wreck furniture before I stick the nail to you."

His features settled into a self-satisfied leer, pleased with his own cleverness, certain he had her. Easing his stance confidently, he tilted slightly back on his heels, and with the movement Meredith saw an opening.

She feinted left toward the living room, then quickly spun around. Her fingers caught the table's edge, a quick balancing touch to propel her weight the opposite way, toward the opening into the kitchen. Beyond that lay the back door and escape outside, where neighbors could hear a scream.

Meredith made one step toward that hope before her arm was yanked backward. He had lunged, his chest tilting over the table's surface, and a viselike grip clamped her wrist.

Meredith felt her body slung backward toward the table's edge. The impact shot pain into her hip, but she braced her feet and threw her weight backward before the iron grip circling her wrist could pull her fully onto the table.

As her head jerked upward, she caught Ed's gaze. His eyes gleamed at first, in mute surprise that he had actually caught her, then their look turned icy as he gave a low, satisfied chuckle.

"Right this way, girl." He gave a tug toward the end of the table. "Come to Ed."

Meredith yanked and twisted, but his hand was locked shut over her flesh. She braced herself against the pressure that wanted to draw her along the side of the table until their bodies would meet at the opposite end. Ed tried levering her arm downward, but her other hand found a grip on the far table edge. He shifted to get a knee up onto the clothed surface, to reach her by crossing it, but a flicker of doubt dimmed his face. If he climbed across after her, she could easily throw him off balance.

Her wrist burned where his grip had rasped it and icy heat radiated up her arm. It was a chill as cold as if some foul, icy fluid were being injected where his fingers touched her. She spun and threw her whole weight into yanking against that grip, but it would not break. His glittering stare watched her, and she knew at once that he was only waiting.

She would tire, he knew that. Already her arm was growing numb. It shot spears of pain up her neck, draining her strength into freezing depths of terror. It was cold, cold, and getting colder. Meredith stood, feeling a sudden draft around her ankles as night air swirled through the coldness of the house. The walls seemed covered with the slick sheen of ice.

Meredith fought against the chill that wanted to penetrate her skin. Determined not to let it inside, she struck back, jamming her hand toward Ed's belly, then twisting away, her shoulder throbbing with pain as she flung her wrist sideways against the angle of his elbow. Her hand suddenly sprang free.

Ed gave a roar and lunged again, but she had two steps on him already and headed for the door to the kitchen. Cold still swirled through her veins, and a chill draft rose from the floor. Ed had caught his balance now and his next long stride would enable him to meet her at the doorway. Meredith darted back toward the wall again.

Then a sound came from behind Ed, in a place where Ed should not be, and in the instant she heard it, Meredith recognized that click, the front door latch, followed by a solid thud. Warm relief rushed over her. It was the front door, the familiar sound of its latch closing. Gus. Gus had to be out there.

"Where are you, Meredith?" Gus's voice seemed like a calm pool, a voice of reason and good sense. It was not urgent. Gus was in control. "Go to the kitchen," Gus said to Arthur. "I'll check upstairs."

Meredith heard steps moving toward the kitchen, but then Gus spoke again. "This place is colder than a tomb." Someone else's voice murmured.

"I'm here, Gus." Her voice quavered, and she felt too weak to push free of the wall and stand on her own. She sank onto a dining room chair, staring up into the eyes and toward the outstretched hands of Ed Johnson.

"I told you so," she whispered. "I told you to leave."

"It's my word against yours," Ed whispered back. "You can't prove shit." He sat down in a chair across from her like an old friend, or like a neighbor who had dropped by to chat. He still did not seem to see the black walls or feel the cold. When Arthur and Gus entered the room he actually grinned at them.

Then he stopped grinning. The shadow moved in the kitchen. "You're under arrest," a voice said. "We've heard enough."

"Not if I get to the bastard first." It was Richard. Richard's face, beautiful and filled with fury, appeared behind the two uniformed men. He shouldered them aside and tried to spring toward Ed, but fell sideways as a policeman grabbed his arm. "Hold it, bud," the policeman said, "or so help me, I'll cuff you." He looked almost serenely at Gus. "Good thing you sent him through the back way with us. We had hell's own time keeping this guy quiet."

Meredith rose unsteadily to go to Richard. She did not

know how he had come here. He looked nearly ready to
fight the police in order to get at Ed. Meredith walked
toward him, and she felt nearly in a trance.

"I tried calling," he said to her, his tone softening but
his eyes still bright with fury. "The line was busy, then
you didn't answer. That was yesterday. But you're all
right, thank God. I left a message with Sally. Didn't she
leave you a note?"

"When Arthur called," Gus said, moving farther into
the room, "I took the liberty of phoning for help." He
stood easily as the two policemen moved toward Ed,
then stopped. When Richard tried to move forward, one
of the policemen shoved him back. "Take care of your
wife," the policeman said. "Let us take care of this."

She stood holding Richard, and he held her. She felt
him tremble with anger, even as he reassured her again
that he had tried to call. He had wanted to let her know
the meeting had ended early and he was coming home.

Meredith half-listened, but concentrated on holding
him close, letting the warmth of his body flow into her
own. She told herself that no matter what else happened,
she must not let go of Richard. He would kill Ed. He
would surely do it. Meredith tried to speak, tried to hold
back tears, and it was her tears that kept Richard away
from Ed. He held her closely and watched as forces in
the house began to shape into a final expression of
darkness and ice.

One of the policemen was very young, obviously not
long on the force. The other was in his mid-thirties, an
experienced man. As the forces in the house changed,
rapidly gathered, and came together in fury, the policemen stood helpless. This should have been a routine
arrest for them. Their puzzled faces showed fear and

indignation. Then the younger policeman's face showed terror.

"And so this does not end it," Gus said sadly. He shivered and reached to touch Meredith's cold hand. "This unhappy affair is not yet over."

Chapter 29

Looking back on what happened—as Meredith certainly did look back during the waking moments of the year that followed—she often wondered how matters would have gone if Elsa had not chosen that exact moment to appear. During that year Meredith's dreams were routine. Lying beside Richard each night during the early months, feeling his nearness and warmth, and feeling their child growing inside her, she once more learned to welcome sleep. She knew that her mind was suppressing a great deal of what she had seen, but she remembered enough.

And, she told herself, it was inevitable that Elsa would show up. Richard's cab had pulled up out front, and there were four cars in the driveway: hers, Arthur's, Gus's, and a police car. That kind of activity would draw Elsa out like a moth to flame.

What she remembered most was ungoverned violence. She could not suppress that part. She remembered the cold, the awful twisting of faces, and the dreadful waves of vengeance that swept the rooms, causing even Gus to recoil. Most of all, she could not forget the violence.

It started with puzzlement. The policemen stood as

helpless as everyone else. The older one tried to take a
step toward Ed Johnson. As he moved he fumbled for his
handcuffs. The younger officer stood frozen.

Then the older policeman stopped, and fear crossed
his face. The fear was mixed with disbelief. He looked at
his feet, as if he wondered why they no longer worked.
He was held in place. "I don't know what in hell is
happening," he muttered to his partner, "but don't jump
into it." He dropped his hand away from the useless
handcuffs.

Through the rooms, layers of cold moved about them,
and the cold carried sobs that were testimony to the death
of dreams. Walls glowered, glazed black as the darkest
anger. Stench rode on the waves of coldness, the fumes
of booze and the smell of fright. Meredith stood transfixed. She willed herself to move but could not. She
could not leave Richard's arms. It was simply that when
she willed movement, her will was overridden. From
deep in her mind came awareness that it was best to not
even try to move. It was best to stand quietly, because
matters were beyond her control.

Footsteps sounded from outside, and another shadow
moved into the kitchen. She recognized Elsa's huffing
and puffing before she even appeared. "I must
say . . . ," Elsa began as she stepped from the kitchen
into the dining room. "I must say . . ."

She stopped, her wide girth filling the doorway as
hands with stubby fingers went to her lips. Her mouth
moved, but no sounds came. She leaned against the
doorway, collecting herself. Her mouth continued to
move. If the rest of them could not will their legs to take
a step, it seemed that Elsa could not will herself to even
make a sound. She concentrated, obviously adding up
everything she saw. Ed Johnson still sat at the table. Gus

and Arthur stood in the background. The two policemen stood before the table, like mannequins arranged for a display.

"Welcome to the show," Ed Johnson croaked. Of all of them, he seemed the least afraid. Meredith wondered if it was whiskey courage or if Ed was still running a bluff.

"Let us not forget," Gus said, "that there are also things of beauty in this house. They were here once, before the violence, and they have returned with Meredith. Let us not forget the beauty." He spoke not to the assembled people, but into the dark waves of coldness and stench.

Forces in the rooms hesitated, seeming to acknowledge Gus's words, and then rose even stronger. Faint and far away, like the echo of an echo, music ran like a tiny voice of hope. The music existed apart from the darkness, but it insisted that it had its place. Gus bowed his head. "It is important to remember all of it," he said. "And it is true that I do not understand vengeance."

It was then that Ed Johnson was tugged, pulled upward, staggering one step toward the living room. His head bobbed, recoiled, and then he braced himself. He was still experiencing no terror, only some confusion. The tugging was steady and not too hard—not yet. Meredith watched Ed's face. It was blank at first. Then, as gradually as if it were blurring on a film screen, it began to contort until it resembled the grotesque grimace of a rubbery mask.

She looked downward to escape the sight of it and saw, above his open collar, the smallest indentations in the flesh, as if Ed's neck were encircled by a noose. Ed grinned, contorting the ghoulish twisting that already marred his lips, perhaps trying to dispel his sense of doom, trying to pretend that he was still in control. Elsa leaned against the doorway, and her lips moved as she gave a rapid lecture. No sounds came, and although Elsa's face showed that the lecture was supercilious, her eyes displayed fear.

Another tug. This time Ed stumbled. He resisted, then took two short steps. His hands went to his throat, and the false courage left his eyes. He fumbled at his throat, gasped, then stood breathing heavily as he was released. He tried to turn, to run away. As he turned, he looked at Elsa.

Her eyes were cold. She watched him as she might critically watch the play of children. She looked at him the way she might look at a newspaperboy who had tossed her paper on the lawn instead of onto the porch. Elsa disclaimed Ed with her eyes. He mouth moved, soundless. She seemed to be saying that she did not even know Ed, much less approve of him.

Another tug. This one short and sharp. Ed staggered, his huge bulk bumping against the doorframe of the living room. The indentations in his neck became deeper, then relaxed. He choked, tried to scream, but could only gasp for breath. His eyes showed horror, but the rest of his face was molded more deeply now, pinched violently into a gargoylelike mask. He was being dragged forward like a man being led to a gallows.

"Please," Meredith whispered. "Don't."

Richard seemed trying to move forward, but could not. Arthur and Gus stood quietly, and Elsa was silent. Arthur tried to step toward Meredith, and she could not tell if his compassion was for her or for Ed.

"There must be no more death in this house," Gus said.

The force hesitated, giving Ed little tugs like a dog

trained to heel on a choke chain. The force seemed to be considering Gus's words.

Gus attempted to step forward to interfere, but was stopped. The older policeman made one step and was stopped. "We do not act beyond the law," Gus said, then fell silent. His hand slipped to his jacket pocket and withdrew his unlighted pipe. "Foolishness," he muttered, "to speak of law with that which obeys other laws." He looked at Richard, then at Meredith. "No matter what happens," he said to Richard, "you must not let Meredith see this. Do not follow. Do not watch."

Light wind rose through the rooms, twisting layers of cold around them. Elsa moved slowly forward, pushed, not tugged, by an invisible but inexorable hand. As she passed Meredith her eyes became cold with blame. Her mouth moved, no doubt saying that this was all Meredith's fault, all Meredith's wickedness. The wind rose, and the front door slammed open. The loud crash startled Ed from his amazement, and he began to fight.

He was a big man, and he fought hard. Each step across the living room saw him resist as the invisible noose tightened. His hands grasped at his throat, then defiantly flailed into darkness and cold. His eyes bulged, and blood began to gather at the corners of his eyes. Blood from lungs that must be tearing apart began to show in the corners of his mouth, rimming his nostrils. He fought, gasped for breath, and blood stained his shirt front as he was dragged through the open door. As he disappeared into darkness, forces in the house relaxed. Meredith found that she could move.

"Stay with Meredith and Richard," Gus said to Arthur. "Keep them out of this." As he spoke, Elsa was slowly shoved forward. She was placed in the doorway, watching Ed in the darkness.

From outside the house, between sobs and screams, came sounds of Ed choking. Sounds rose in the night; they were torn and racking sounds; sobs, attempted shrieks, pale voices of fear turned to horror and anguish. Whatever was killing Ed was taking its time. The policemen moved quickly, pushing past Elsa, but Meredith did not hear their footsteps get past the front porch. The police were yelling commands but no one was listening. There were only the hideous gasps, the slow choking, the thrashing of a body that was now surely on all fours, fighting darkness and death.

Gus moved toward the doorway, standing behind Elsa and looking over her shoulder. She turned to him, and her mouth formed in the shape of a scream but no sound came. Gus watched, and then trembled. He braced himself against the doorframe, his body rigid. Meredith could not believe that Gus would ever react that way. Gus stood for strength, for rationality, for hope. Seeing him that way made her understand the depth of terror she had carried for weeks.

Chokes faded to gasps, and gasps faded to silence before sounds of ripping slit through the darkness. This was not like the tearing of paper, but muffled; soft, yet furious. Meredith heard small snaps from breaking bones, and muffled ripping and tearing hovered in the mist.

Then there were gasps of shock; but these gasps were not from Ed. A policeman tried to speak as sounds of fury rose in the darkness.

"My God," Gus whispered. "Let no one ever again die such a death as that." In horror, he backed away from the doorway, where Elsa remained transfixed.

"Get to the car radio," the older policeman croaked to the younger one. "Get some backup here. Move." Then his voice faltered. "I've seen the worst traffic wrecks in the world, but nothing . . ."

More choking. Gasps. A whisper. "All those things out there are dead. Why don't they stop moving?" Then the younger voice choked off as hard sounds of retching turned into sounds of the young policeman vomiting. "Puke and get over it," the older policeman said. "I think I'm gonna join you."

Red and blue lights of emergency vehicles flashed in front of the house as a coroner's truck departed. Neighbors stood in the mist along the chill sidewalk. There was a fire truck out there, and sounds of spraying water told Meredith that fire hoses were covering the lawn. What the police could not explain, they were washing away. That seemed almost sensible.

She had sat in numb silence at the dining room table with Richard beside her. Action and voices swirled. Her mind had retreated. She felt small and still, like a fearful child hiding from the wrath of adults. For a while Gus also sat beside her. Then, at a hurried call from Arthur, Gus went to the living room to help Elsa.

"This is not normal shock," Gus said to Arthur. From the dining room Meredith remotely understood that Elsa lay on the couch as the two men attended to her. "Of course she's in shock," Gus said, "but there are physical manifestations beyond shock."

"I think she can't hear you," Arthur said. "She can't move her arms or legs, and I think she can't hear."

"Something is wrong," Meredith told Richard. "I have to help."

"Don't count on it," he said grimly, "and don't go in there. Trust Gus."

"She may regain movement," Gus said about Elsa.

"But you are right about her hearing. I think she hears nothing but her own voice."

"I can't hear a word she says."

"Doctors will examine her," Gus told Arthur, but it looks like there is no physical damage." Then his voice sank to a mutter. "The mind can play tricks, but I'm not sure her mind has. To tell the truth, I'm not sure of anything."

And so that was it, Meredith thought. She knew, somehow, something she would never say to Gus. This was the punishment laid on Elsa by a violent and vengeful force. Elsa would never, ever hear a single sound except the sound of her own voice, Meredith was sure, but no one else would ever hear that voice. Meredith thought of the many, many words that came from Elsa. She thought of the spite, the petty machinations, the triviality, and small nastiness of Elsa. Meredith was not sure that Ed had received the worst punishment.

"The ambulance is coming," Arthur said.

"See to it," Gus said. "Then join us. In a while I'll make coffee." He left the living room and returned to Meredith, to sit beside her, holding her hand. "That took immeasurable courage," he said to her. "Few people have such courage."

She was not sure what he meant, and she did not feel courageous. She only felt that she had done what was necessary to protect all of them.

"You caught Richard out front? To think he almost walked in on that plan I had Arthur call you about."

"Good thing Gus saw me get out of the cab," Richard answered for him. "And he made me wait. He's the best friend we'll ever have." He looked up as Arthur entered the room. Meredith was weak, but managed to stand.

·

"I'm a little bit wobbly," she said to Gus, "but it's over now."

"It probably isn't," Gus said, "but the darkness has passed." He reached to steady her, saw that she was in control. He pulled his pipe from his jacket and tamped tobacco from a pouch. "The circle must close," he muttered, "and it has not closed yet."

As if in answer, a faint light began to rise from the shadows. It was not normal light, but it was not threatening. Gold luminosity tinged the air. A sense of finality and acceptance surrounded them, and Meredith immediately understood that the forces that held Patty now released her. The game was played, horror added to horror, but now Patty was free.

In Meredith's memory Patty appeared, for minutes or for only an instant. Meredith could never say, but time made no difference to the importance of the memory.

"Let us not forget that there are also things of beauty in this house." Gus had said that. When he had spoken those words, the forces of cold and stench had hesitated. Now beauty spread through the rooms, and it would be beauty that would draw the final curtain.

The four clustered together: Gus, Meredith, Richard, and Arthur. Then Arthur was gently detached from the group. A bare hint of music moved through the light, felt more than heard. Arthur's eyes filled with tears, and his face showed a curious mixture of grief and joy.

Arthur stepped toward the once-familiar living room as music surrounded him. The presence that filled the house was not apologetic. It was loving and it carried regret, but it no longer held fear or loneliness. Arthur stood in the great solitude of his memories and grief, and it seemed to Meredith that for a while he was joined to another presence. Soft light covered him, focused on him, and he was surrounded by a gentle love that was no longer timid.

Meredith turned away then, as did Gus. They left Arthur in the great privacy of farewell, but Meredith hesitated, as it seemed to her that she was momentarily included. She felt the gentle passage of Patty being released, and also felt a quick and private whisper as Patty placed a blessing on her house.